Winning Means Everything!

"Michael Pierce had better not mess with me," I told Allison as we got off the bus. "And he'd better not win that contest."

"Honestly, I wish you wouldn't get so upset," Allison said.

"I'm going to win the contest and get my parents back together, and nobody is going to stop me." I stomped up the steps and headed toward our classroom.

Behind me I heard Allison call out, but I didn't bother turning around. "Give me a break," she said. "I'm trying to be your friend."

I ducked my head as I headed into our classroom. Nobody understood. Nobody would ever understand. Without Dad, life was a big forehead full of zits.

Elaine Moore

If you purchased this book without a cover, you should be aware that this book is stolen property. It was reported as "unsold and destroyed" to the publisher, and neither the author nor the publisher has received any payment for this "stripped book."

Text copyright © 1997 by Elaine Moore.

Cover illustration by Jeff Mangiat.
Copyright © 1997 by Troll Communications L.L.C.

Published by Troll Communications L.L.C.

All rights reserved. No part of this book may be reproduced or utilized in any form or by any means, electronic or mechanical, including photocopying, recording, or by any information storage and retrieval system, without written permission from the publisher.

Printed in the United States of America.

10 9 8 7 6 5 4 3 2 1

Contents

For Dave

Chapter 1

My Dad

The first thing you should know about Reid Kulik, my dad, is that he is handsome—movie star, model handsome. If he wanted, he could be on any of the soaps. And I'm not the only one who says so. At one time or another practically every girl in my fifth-grade class has had a crush on my father, including my best friend, Allison Lampe, although she would never admit it now. Last Christmas even snooty Deidra Carroll offered me five dollars just so she could ice-skate with him at our community's New Year's Eve party.

Naturally I turned her down, and that's the second thing you should know. When I am with my dad, he makes me feel as if I am the most special person in the whole wide world. I don't share him with anyone, not for a million dollars, unless, of course, it's with my mom.

My mom and I waited as long as we could for Dad

to come home on New Year's Eve. Finally we went to the ice rink. Since my dad drives a taxi, I figured he had a late fare to National Airport, or maybe even Baltimore, and got tangled up in traffic. It wouldn't have been the first time.

By eleven o'clock I was on the ice and resting against the rails, trying to be casual as I checked the designer watch Dad gave me for Christmas. What was taking him so long anyway?

Meanwhile Deidra was hanging all over me, pestering. Allison and I tried to dodge her, but every time we turned around, Deidra was in my face, demanding, "Where's your father? Where's your father?"

I glanced over my shoulder toward the double doors that separated the rink from the warming area. Any minute I expected the doors to burst open with a loud boom as my father strode toward all of us. Instead a familiar sick feeling began creeping through my stomach.

Just then Mike Pierce zoomed through the crowd of skaters circling the ice and did an impressive hockey stop three inches in front of my toe. His blue eyes shone. His cheeks were like apples.

"Hey, rink rat! I thought you came here to skate. Forget about your dad. It's obvious he's not coming."

That was when I slammed into Mike as hard as I could, sending him sprawling across the ice.

Chapter 2

Happy New Year

"Hey, how's my girl?"

When Dad finally came home, I was in bed. Down the hall I could hear Mom banging pots and pans around in the kitchen. She always reorganized her cabinets when she was angry with my father.

I rolled over, ignoring him.

"Aw, Stephie," he pleaded, "don't be like that. I can explain."

I sat up fast. "Yeah? Then where were you? You were supposed to be at the ice rink. New Year's Eve, remember? All the kids in town and their folks were there. Everyone was there except you, and you promised!"

"Hey," he said, looking over his shoulder as if maybe he didn't want Mom to hear, "you know how it is on New Year's Eve."

I thumped my pillow and folded my arms across my chest. I didn't care if it was New Year's Eve. "You still should have been at the ice rink," I said, glaring at him.

"Something told me you wouldn't understand. C'mon, Stephie, my heart is breaking." It took him only two steps, and he was at my window. He gave the shade a tug, and it snapped sharply all the way to the top. "C'mon, Stephie," he said again. "Look out the window. I left the porch light on so you could see. I got us a limousine."

He got us a *limousine*? How could I not look? I scrambled out of bed. There against the curb was the longest, shiniest, whitest, brightest car I'd ever seen in my life.

"C'mon, what are you waiting for?"

"What about Mom?" I asked, suddenly not sure.

Again Dad glanced over his shoulder. "Nah, this is for us. I want to start the new year off with a date with my best girl."

Before I could say a word, he had draped his jacket over my shoulders and plunked one of his old baseball caps on my head. Suddenly it was easy to forget how he'd disappointed me only hours before. I followed him down the hallway in my bedroom slippers, feeling like Cinderella going to the ball.

But waiting for us in the living room, my mother had other ideas.

"Reid, grow up! You cannot take Stephanie out. It feels like snow, and she's not even dressed properly. For pete's sake, it's after two o'clock in the morning!"

"We'll just go around the block. Nothing fancy. A test drive. We'll be home before you have your skillets sorted. I want Stephie to see how smooth the limo runs."

"This can't wait until tomorrow?" she said, ignoring the crack about her pots and pans.

My father took a deep breath. "Look, Lisa, we both know what's happening tomorrow. She's my daughter too."

I could see my mother fuming. "You should have been at the party."

"Hey, not you too! Look, I've got a right—"

"Reid, not now." My mother sighed. "Stephanie, you can go, but put on some decent clothes."

I started toward my room. Behind me they were still arguing.

"I want Stephanie home in—"

"Thirty minutes?"

"Since when does it take a half hour to go around the block?"

"Okay, five," my dad said. "Are you satisfied?"

"Five."

"Whose car is it?" I asked once we were outside with the front door shut behind us. I rubbed my arms. Even wearing jeans and a sweatshirt under Dad's jacket, I was still cold.

I could feel Mom watching us through the bay window.

The porch light was still on. I knew it would stay on until I was back home.

"Not a car, Steph. A limousine, and it's mine."

My eyes rested briefly on the shiny boomerang thing on the trunk that my dad said was a TV antenna. My breath was coming out in little clouds. "What about your cab?"

"Traded it in."

I didn't know a lot about cars, but I knew that a cab didn't cost nearly as much as a limousine. I also knew my dad didn't have enough money to buy a limousine.

"Can we afford it?"

"Shh. You sound like your mother." He put his finger to his lips. "C'mon. You want to say hello to your friends?"

"Dad! They're asleep."

He held the door open, and I ducked my head as I climbed inside. "Wow! We could bowl in here! Where do I sit?"

"You're the princess. You can sit wherever you want to sit."

"Okay," I said, pointing. "I'll sit way back there."

"Great. Let me fold the other seats down." He slammed the seats together. "There! Now you have a nice table."

"Neat, Dad."

The seats were soft leather. So what if they were cold? I pulled my legs up underneath me and breathed on my hands. When Dad got in behind the steering wheel, he was at least a half-mile away.

"It'll take a little while for the heat to reach you back there. The heater needs to be fixed," he hollered as he pulled slowly away from the curb. "I'll leave this privacy window open."

I shivered and hoped the heat would hurry up and come on in the back of the car.

"You might be able to get the television working if you play around with it. Go ahead and try it."

"What about the phone?" I shouted back.

"I have to get it serviced. Is it warm back there yet?"

"No. Is that a refrigerator?"

He laughed, obviously pleased that I'd noticed. That's another thing about my father. When he laughs, he brightens even the darkest night. I was beginning to forgive him for not showing up at the ice rink.

"Yeah. Open it up," he said. "I got you a surprise."

Surprise? I loved Dad's surprises. And any surprise inside a limousine would have to be fantastic. I scooted across the table and gave the refrigerator handle a hard jerk.

It was a surprise all right. Inside were two cans of Dad's favorite beer, all that was left of a six-pack. It didn't take a genius to figure out that while Mom and I had been waiting for Dad, he'd been having his own party.

"Steph, did you find it?"

I shoved the stupid beer to the side. The candy bar was in the back.

"Found it."

"See! Would I forget my girl? Hey, I've had enough of this going around the block. What's that smart kid's name?" he asked. "The one who always wins everything?"

"Mike Pierce?"

"That's it. Bet he never won a limousine ride. He lives on Blair Avenue, right? White house, green shutters?"

Blair Avenue wasn't exactly around the block, but since we were still on the same side of town, I guessed it wouldn't matter. When we got to Mike's house, Dad pulled into the circular driveway and beeped his horn.

I couldn't help myself. I was laughing so hard I could have died. When the porch lights flashed on, I forgot the limousine had tinted windows, and I crouched down on the floor so nobody would see me.

Then Dad stepped on the accelerator, and we zoomed off like a rocket, roaring through the neighborhood for three, five, seven blocks. At the intersection he didn't wait for the green light before turning onto Maple Avenue.

"Mom's going to kill us," I yelled.

"Trust me," Dad said dryly. "She won't kill both of us. And if she were going to kill me, she'd have done it a long time ago."

Maybe it was the way he said it. Or maybe it was because suddenly being Cinderella in a fancy coach wasn't much fun without a Prince Charming. Or maybe it was because the heat still hadn't reached me in the backseat. Whatever the reason, I didn't wait to be invited. I crawled through the privacy window to sit beside him in the front.

"Hey, kiddo."

"You don't mind, do you?" I tried not to shiver. I didn't want to hurt his feelings. "I'd really rather sit here."

"Great." He tapped my knee. "Because I'm going to make this a night you won't ever forget. A special New Year's Eve date in beautiful downtown Washington, D.C., with my best girl."

First we rode around all the monuments and museums, which were lit up and much prettier at night. We drove past the huge national Christmas tree with its sparkling bulbs and zillion glittering lights. Then we were in Georgetown. I'd been there with Mom but never at night. I couldn't believe all the people milling around as though it were daytime.

Suddenly my father stopped. He jumped out of the limo and ran to where a man dressed as a gorilla was selling balloons filled with sparkly confetti. Back in the front seat, it was my dad and me and three bobbing confetti-filled balloons.

He threw back his head and laughed. "I love the expression on your face!"

I was so confused. Half of me felt overwhelmed by his attention, but the other half felt bruised by my earlier disappointment at the ice rink, especially now that I knew about the missing four cans of beer. Nonetheless, I didn't want the evening ever to end.

We were on our way home, going over the beautiful Memorial Bridge, when my father said, "This evening is going to have to last us for a long time, Stephie. Tomorrow I'm packing up this buggy. Your mom and I . . ." He paused. "We're calling it quits."

Maybe, with all their fighting, I should have expected it. Maybe I should have understood. But when you were riding around in a limousine at night with your father and three bobbing balloons, it was more than you should be expected to understand.

"Why? Where are you going?"

"Steph, your mom . . . she doesn't understand. I wanted to leave earlier. What's the sense in dragging it out, I said, but she thought we should stick it out until after the holidays. You know, give you a nice Christmas. Besides, I didn't have the deal worked out on the limousine."

"But where are you going? What are you going to do?"

"I thought I'd try Florida. Orlando. Like in the commercials, I'm going to Disney World."

If it was supposed to be a joke, it wasn't funny.

"There's plenty to see down there," he continued. "Tourists all year round. Business won't have slow spots the way it does here. And it won't be cold. I won't have to worry about getting this heater fixed."

Won't have to worry about . . . "Can I go too?" I blurted.

"Steph." Dad cleared his throat. "It's just me, Steph."

"Oh." There had to be some mistake. "Until you find the right place, right? Then we'll come too. Right? I'll bet you'll get free passes to Disney World and everything."

The lights along the side of the highway whipped past, making a cardboard mask out of the side of Dad's face. When he didn't answer, I started getting nervous.

Suddenly I didn't care that he'd missed my skating party. Or why. I didn't care what the other kids said. What did they know anyway? I didn't care that sometimes he forgot my birthday. When someone had to remember the roads to every airport and every bridge and all those important buildings and one-way streets, it was easy to see how he could forget a birthday. I didn't care about any of those things. I just wanted Dad to fill up the silence by saying something I wanted to hear.

"Stephie, I won't be looking for a place that big."

"It doesn't have to be big," I insisted. "I'm just a kid. I don't take up much space. I can sleep on the couch."

Vienna was dark and empty as we quietly rolled down the street. The traffic lights blinked their red eyes, and this time Dad stopped at every one. All I wanted was to go home to my bed, so I could cover my head with my pillow and pretend that what he'd said was a bad dream. Something told me it wasn't going to be that simple.

When we got home, Mom was in her robe, waiting in the living room. I had never seen her so mad.

"Where in the world have you been?" she shouted at Dad. "I've been worried to death." Then, turning to me, "Stephanie, are you all right?"

She knelt on the floor, peering into my face as though she couldn't believe it was actually me.

"I'm fine, Mom. Honest."

"Oh, for God's sake, Lisa, don't be so dramatic. We've been out on the town." He let go of the balloons. As they floated toward the ceiling, he popped one with his keys. Confetti flew all over the place.

"Honestly, Reid, that isn't funny. I don't call what's happening here a celebration. Mrs. Pierce called after you woke the neighborhood with your juvenile antics. That was two hours ago. This is exactly why . . . I should have known better than to let you—"

Then she turned and saw me standing there, watching and hearing everything.

I didn't wait. I turned my back on them and headed toward my bedroom.

A few minutes later the front door slammed. Mom came immediately to my room and sat beside me on my bed.

"It's my fault you're mad at Dad," I said. "I shouldn't have gone."

Mom didn't let me say any more. She hugged me. "Oh, no, sweetie. Don't think that. Not ever. It wasn't just tonight."

"Why then?" I demanded, pulling away. "Tell me why you and Dad are splitting up? I want to know."

"There are lots of reasons." I had to strain to hear. "Too many problems. Your father and I . . ."

"Can't you work them out?"

"Oh, honey, we've tried."

"Well, can't you try harder?"

"Stephanie, sometimes, it's . . ." She put her hands up to her face, and her shoulders started to shake.

"He says he's going to Florida, Mom."

"I know," Mom sobbed.

The next day, New Year's Day, I watched Dad carry box after box out to the curb and stuff everything into the limo. It was really sad. With the doors shut and the windows rolled up, the shiny white limousine was the most beautiful car I'd ever seen. Yet inside that shiny white limousine, Dad had crammed everything he ever owned or cared about except Mom and me.

When Dad put the last box in the trunk, I glanced back toward the house. I kept hoping the door would fly open and Mom would come running down the sidewalk to beg Dad not to leave.

Or maybe we all should pack our suitcases and get

a head start on a vacation in sunny Florida.

But none of that happened. When my dad finished arranging the cardboard boxes across the floor and the backseat of the limousine, he said, "See ya around, Steph. I'll give you a call when I find out where I'm staying."

I gave him a good long hug.

"I want you to be brave now. No crying. Your old man can't take that."

"Aren't you going to say good-bye to Mom?"

"She knows I'm leaving."

"Dad?"

He didn't answer. Instead he climbed into the car and started the engine. Suddenly the window gave a funny little clink and rolled down.

"Here." He handed me a brochure. "This is the tour company where I'll be working. They'll know how to reach me."

I know it sounds strange, but none of this seemed real until he put that brochure in my hand. Maybe it was the green map of Florida with the bright yellow sun where Orlando was supposed to be. Maybe it was the picture of Mickey and Minnie, the waving white hands. I flung my arms around Dad and buried my head in his neck. He was wearing the aftershave lotion I got him for Christmas.

"Oh, Stephie." His voice broke. "You know how I love you." He kissed me on the tip of my nose.

He was probably afraid he was going to start

crying too, because he reached for the window button. I stepped back and took a deep breath as snowflakes, big as tissues, began drifting out of the sky. When Dad drove his white limo up and over the hill, the only thing I could think was that he was going to Disney World without us.

Chapter 3

The Contest

I started writing my dad the day after he left. At first it was pretty hard getting to "Your loving daughter" without breaking the point on my pencil at least a half dozen times. Finally I wised up and began using a pen—a metal ballpoint because felt tips mashed flat in no time and the plastic kind always cracked. It had to be waterproof too, because if I wasn't careful, a runaway tear would plop in the middle of the page and ruin everything. I might tell Dad how angry and hurt I was at him for leaving us, but I sure as heck wasn't going to send him something that looked as if it had sat out in the rain.

I wrote him practically around the clock. Sometimes in the morning before meeting Allison at the bus stop. Sometimes in school when I finished a math test ahead of everyone else. Sometimes while watching TV or before going to bed. But mostly I wrote the letters at Allison's house, which was where

Mom said I had to go after school now that she was working at Home D-Cor in addition to taking classes at our local community college.

Mom's going back to college on top of working wasn't something she'd planned any more than she'd planned Dad's leaving. And she didn't decide to do it without talking it over with me first. Since old Mrs. DeSanto, the owner of Home D-Cor, offered to pay Mom's tuition, we decided it wouldn't be too smart for Mom to pass up the opportunity.

Like Mom says, there are a lot of things you can lose in life, but an education is something no one can take away from you. Probably that's why she's careful to check my homework every night before sitting down at the kitchen table and doing her own.

At first Mom said having Mrs. DeSanto pay her tuition was too much like charity. Then Mrs. DeSanto said the only thing that was keeping her from going to Europe was Home D-Cor. If she had someone reliable to manage the store, she'd be gone in a heartbeat. *Reliable* could be my mom's middle name.

In two months' time we'd made some pretty big changes. It would have been nice knowing what Dad was up to. It was as if he didn't want us to know where he was. But then, I reasoned every time I stuffed a letter inside an envelope and addressed it to him in care of the post office box for Sunshine Tours, any minute he might come home, where he belonged.

By the middle of March I'd written an awful lot of

letters. Maybe 250 or so. Dad hadn't written back once.

"Maybe he's not getting them," I told Allison. We were in her room as usual. She was lying on her stomach on her bed while I sat on the floor, knees up, my back against the wall, notebook in front of me, metal ballpoint in my hand.

Allison gave me a knowing look. "My mom says if he wasn't, they would have been returned."

"So I guess he's getting them then."

"Unless," Allison said slowly, "that dead mailman in McLean got your letters." Allison had a way of looking at the bright side of things.

"What dead mailman? How could a dead mailman get my letters?"

"No, silly! The mailman was lying dead in his apartment for a whole week." Allison's finger stabbed the air. "Finally, when he started to stink, the landlady opened the door with her key and called the police. They found his gross decayed body, and they also found a whole bunch of undelivered mail stuffed in every closet in the apartment. It was on the news. He had never delivered that mail. A whole bunch of people never got their bills. It could happen, Steph."

"No such luck. Unless you think there could be two dead mailmen. Remember, I sent Dad a postcard when Mom and I were visiting Aunt Milly in Baltimore for my eleventh birthday. He didn't answer that either."

Allison scooted off the bed. "I can't stand it. C'mon, we're supposed to go to the store for my mom. Besides, it's too gruesome watching you write letters all the time." She stopped. "You know, your mom really wants to talk to him."

The pen fell from my hand and rolled across the floor. "To my dad? How do you know?"

Allison shrugged. "I heard her telling my mom."

I couldn't believe Allison hadn't told me right away. What was the big secret? "Where was I?"

"Where you always are, goofhead. Up here writing letters."

"What did she say? I mean, *exactly*."

"Exactly." Allison paused dramatically. "'If I could just talk to Reid.' But it was the way she said it. Oh, Steph, you should have heard it for yourself. Your mom sounded really desperate."

"Like maybe she wants him back?"

"All I know is what I heard."

"What else? Why didn't you come get me?"

"Nothing else, and I couldn't come get you. Matthew started crying, and Mom wanted me to be a nice big sister and play with him. I think they had more grown-up talk, which I couldn't hear because Matthew kept crying for his blanket."

"When was this? I still can't believe you didn't tell me."

"It was last week, I guess. Anyway I thought you knew."

"How could I? My mom refuses to say anything about my dad. Nothing! It's one big zero!"

"Well, it sure sounded to me like she desperately wants to talk to your dad."

"Wow." I stuck my unfinished letter in my pocket. This was the best news I'd heard in a long time.

On the way back from the store Allison and I decided to stop at Mr. Delvechio's for an ice cream.

The sign was propped up on Mr. Delvechio's glass counter. It was bright pink with brown polka dots and huge black lettering that read:

Contest
Invent Our 32nd Flavor
First-place Winner Receives
An All-Expense-Paid Family Vacation
To Disney World

I didn't bother reading the other prizes. I just stood like a zombie. Disney World. Dad!

Mom and I would go on spring break.

Somewhere in the background I could hear Mr. Delvechio. "Maybe Stephanie doesn't like ice cream anymore."

Coming out of my trance, I could see a wrapped cone in his hand, ready for filling.

Allison shifted the bag of groceries she was carrying and nudged me to hurry. Flustered, I scanned the list of flavors hanging on the wall, right under the mural of brown-and-white cows munching grass in the pasture.

Chocolate, chocolate, chocolate. Chocolate what?

I pressed my finger to the glass and announced my flavor, not thinking about anything other than the cool whipped chocolate that would soon be placed against my tongue. Unfortunately, rushing made my voice louder than normal.

"Chocolate mouse," I said in a voice that carried. It didn't occur to me that I'd just asked Mr. Delvechio for a scoop of chocolate rodent.

For a moment no one said anything. Then Mike Pierce stepped behind me and hooted in my ear. "That's the funniest thing I ever heard! Chocolate mouse! Wow! Wait till the guys hear about this!"

Beside me Allison's face was bright red. I was sure mine matched.

"Don't you know *any* French?" Mike exclaimed. "That's *mousse,* not mouse!"

To tell the truth, it made me mad. Just because his mother cooks out of a French cookbook, Mike acts as if he has a patent on the French language.

Mouse. Moose. Mousse. What difference did it make? What was important was the chocolate.

Quickly I corrected myself. "I meant 'mousse,' Mr. Delvechio. A scoop of chocolate mousse." But of course Mr. Delvechio knew what I meant. His arm was already in the right barrel. Only loudmouth Mike would make a big deal out of such a little mistake. I sighed all the way down to my sneakers, remembering the first and most rotten thing about Mike was his big mouth. Tomorrow the whole fifth grade would know about Stephanie and the Chocolate Mouse.

"Is the contest for kids too?" I asked Mr. Delvechio, trying to hide some of my embarrassment.

"Sure is." He capped the cone with a scoop of chocolate mousse and handed it to me. "You have to start by using my vanilla ice cream as a base. After that you can add any ingredients you want. You can enter only once, though, and you have to do it soon. The deadline is April first."

I turned to Allison as I rummaged in my pocket for some money. "This is perfect, Allison. I win the prize, and my mom and I are off to see my dad."

"Great!" Allison exclaimed. "Count me in. I'll help."

"Mr. Delvechio," I said, "I'll take two scoops of your vanilla right now." I nodded my thanks and grabbed a pink entry form from the box beside the poster.

Just then I felt Mike's arm reach over my shoulder. "While you're at it, give me a whole pint," Mike said.

I rolled my eyes at Allison. What a hog. Mike Pierce was entering the contest too.

"I don't care if Mike is entering the contest," I told Allison on the way back to her house. "So what if he always wins everything? Every church raffle. Every science fair. Every bingo game. This time I'm going to win. Nobody, especially Michael Pierce, is going to keep me and my mom from getting together with my dad."

It surprised me how saying it made me even more determined.

"Sure." Allison wasn't convinced. "Just remember his mother has a catering business *and* that fancy super sorbet ice-cream machine. His whole family is like professional food. You can't beat that."

"Phooey," I said. "Mike's not going to stop me. Besides, you can't win unless you try. That's what my mother says." She's right too. I don't like it when people make excuses, like "Oh, I could never do that." How do they know if they don't even try?

"Hey, mouse!" Mike tore past us on his bike, waving his entry form as if he were already holding an all-expense-paid ticket to Disney World.

Instinctively I shouted back, "You're not going to win this time, Mike. I am!"

"I don't think this is going to work," Allison whispered once her mother had left the kitchen. "You need special machines to make ice cream. My mother doesn't like me to use her blender."

I raised my eyebrows. "You've got something better."

"I do?"

I nodded. "The microwave." I opened up a drawer.

"And wooden spoons. All the rules said was to invent the thirty-second flavor using Mr. Delvechio's vanilla. It didn't say how."

Allison shifted her weight to her other hip. "So what are you thinking?"

"All we have to do is put some of the vanilla in a bowl, stick a bunch of neat stuff on top, and nuke it in the microwave. Then we smush everything together with wooden spoons until we come up with a winning combination. That's all."

Making myself at home, I took the cup of ice cream out of the paper bag and set it on the counter. I scooped some into a cereal bowl.

"We might not even have to nuke it. Watch," I said as I began to flatten it with the back of a spoon. "Didn't you ever do this when you were little?" I didn't bother to tell Allison I still did it when my mother wasn't around.

"Oh, gross." Allison groaned.

"It is not gross. It's good," I argued. "Now hand me the chocolate syrup."

Allison did as she was told. "I still think what you're doing is weird."

I didn't pay any attention. I was too busy scanning the interior of Mrs. Lampe's cabinets.

"What goes with chocolate?"

"I'm sure you'd say *everything*," Allison said with a smirk. I ignored her. This was not the time to get into an argument.

"What about more chocolate?" I answered, having spotted an open package of Hershey's chips on the top shelf.

Before Allison could say otherwise, I pressed my palms against the counter and hoisted myself up. I grabbed the bag of chips and dropped lightly to the floor. You would have thought I was a cat burglar, I was so quiet.

"Is it all right if we use this?"

"Sure. But in case you didn't know," Allison said, "chocolate chocolate chip is already invented."

"I know. It's only a test," I said. "We have to try it first on something we know is good. Then we invent something new."

"Great idea."

"Of course," I said. "That's because it's mine."

While Allison watched, I stuck the vanilla ice cream in the microwave until it reached the soft smush stage. Then I stirred in chocolate syrup and a handful of chips. After laying a piece of plastic wrap across the bowl, I slid the whole works in the freezer. I set the oven timer for twenty minutes.

"So what do you think your dad's doing in Florida?" Allison asked as we waited for the timer to ding.

"Probably he's using his new limousine to set up his own sight-seeing business. He always wanted to do that, you know. He was going to drive his own bus, one that he owned, not someone else's. Then someday, after my mom and dad had built their company up, he was going to buy a fleet of limousines and pay people to work for him. I figure this is his way of getting started."

"Oh, yeah? What was it going to be called?"

"Tip Top Tours," I said brightly. "Mom and Dad used to tell me about it all the time. Mom was going to handle the business part while my dad gave the tours." I felt a smile cross my face. "We were going to be the Tip Top Tour Team."

"Why didn't you do it?"

A lump formed in my throat. I stared at my hand as I poured more soda pop into a glass. I noticed that it was shaking.

"Mom says Dad got tired of the idea. They weren't exactly getting along. That's when he quit working for the TourMobile company and started driving taxis. After a while she got tired too. She says some dreams are so big it takes two people to hold them up."

Not knowing what else to say, and careful not to look at Allison, I carried the dishes to the sink.

"Now that Dad has his limousine, I figure that's what he's doing. That's why we haven't heard from him. He's starting Tip Top Tours, but he's doing it without us. My dad really likes to surprise people."

What I didn't tell Allison was that for once I didn't want a surprise—not even a good one. What I wanted was my dad and mom back together the way they belonged. Winning Mr. Delvechio's contest seemed the only way.

When the oven timer finally dinged, the smush was frozen with frosty snow crystals on top of the plastic wrap. Being the good hostess, Allison took two spoons out of a drawer and handed me one.

"Not bad," she said between tastes. "Hey, this is going to be fun."

"What's fun?" Both of us jumped. We'd been so busy eating we hadn't heard Mrs. Lampe come through the dining room to stand by the kitchen door.

"Mr. Delvechio's having a contest." I crossed my fingers and hoped Mrs. Lampe wouldn't ask about the grand prize. "We're inventing a new flavor."

There was the slightest hesitation. Her gaze went from me to Allison. Apparently she didn't notice my discomfort.

"Too bad this one's already been invented," she said, surprising us by dipping a third spoon in the bowl. "It's good. But you girls are going to have to come up with something different. Me, I like crunch in my ice cream."

"Like nuts?" I asked.

"Mmm, more than nuts," Mrs. Lampe said, thinking. "Crunchy and maybe sweeter."

She was trying to be helpful.

"Like peanut brittle. Yes." She nodded, eyes closed and definitely sure of herself. "A taffy-colored ribbon of peanut brittle swirled in rich chocolate ice cream. Try that next. And let me taste it when you do."

I could hardly believe it. Not only had Mrs. Lampe

suggested what might turn out to be the winning flavor, but she'd given Allison and me permission to turn her kitchen into our laboratory. I let another spoonful of chocolate melt against my tongue. Nothing could stop us now. Not even win-it-all Mike Pierce and his super sorbet ice-cream machine.

Chapter 4

Chocolate
Mooo-ooooose

Mom was bent over the kitchen table, sliding tiny scraps of paper across a tablet with fierce, thick black lines drawn in both directions. Her nose was so close to the tabletop she looked as if she might be memorizing the lines with her nostrils.

"Do you think that's a good idea?" I asked. "You might go blind."

She didn't even look up. "It's supposed to be easier this way. See, sweetie." She pointed to a scrap. "This little red rectangle is the couch. This smaller green square is the end table. And I have the living room drawn to scale on the tablet. This is interior decorating with a professional's touch. I might as well practice with my own home."

I shook my head in despair. I ought to be used to it by now.

Mom had been constantly rearranging furniture ever since Dad left. Usually she waited until the weekend to do the heavy stuff, but all week long she was thinking where she'd put the bed next. Should the living-room lamp sit on this table beside the chair, or that table beside the couch? Sometimes her thinking got so strong she didn't make it until Saturday. Sometimes I heard her moving furniture in the middle of the night.

"I wish you'd stop doing this, Mom," I told her one Saturday after walking out of my room and banging into Grandma's antique curio cabinet on my way to the bathroom. "I don't even know my own house anymore."

"Don't be silly, Stephanie. It's the same furniture, and I'm still here. I'm trying for a brighter, less cluttered, more open effect. Don't you like it this way? See, from the couch, you can gaze out the window."

There was no point in arguing. Before the weekend was over, she'd have everything switched around again.

Pillows came next: bright red, gold, tasseled, needlepoint, fuzzy, velvet. They stayed a couple of days, being moved from couch to chair, before being returned to where they belonged, with good old Mrs. DeSanto at Home D-Cor. But as confusing as I found it, Mom thought Mrs. DeSanto and all this redecorating were the best things that had ever happened to her—except for the day that I was born, of course. And maybe the day she and Dad got married.

"Stephanie." Mom's eyes, dark as coal against her

pale face, stared at me. I tried hard not to notice the shadows from lack of sleep. "It just dawned on me what's missing," she said.

I held my breath. Obviously she was going to say Dad.

"We need a bath mat."

My mouth dropped all the way down to my toes. "Bath mat?" I whispered hoarsely. What did a bath mat have to do with Dad?

"As a matter of fact, we're going to redo the whole house," she announced. Before I knew what was happening, she leaped out of her chair and bolted into the living room, where she began waving her arms.

She must have noticed me staring in shock at her unexpected burst of energy. Suddenly she stopped.

"We'll have to start small, of course," she said, sounding more controlled. "One room at a time. And since we don't have much money, the best place to start is with a bath mat. How about yellow? It would give our little bathroom a cheerful note." Mom reached over to hug me. "We both could use a little cheer."

"With a bath mat? Mom, get real."

"You'd be surprised." She was staring into space, probably admiring her cheerful yellow bath mat. I wondered if cheerful bath mats came complete with smiley faces. "I'd like to try wallpaper," Mom said. "Your father never wanted wallpaper, but you should see the samples they bring into class."

I rolled my eyes.

"We could do it together. Of course, papering might be too expensive." She placed a finger against her cheek, thinking. The lines on her forehead deepened. "I'd have to check, but what if we stenciled? We got the cutest little stencils in the store last week." She paused. "We could start with your room."

Stencils? Cute? Little kids like Matthew had cute little stencils in their nurseries: teddy bears and blocks.

"Mom, don't do anything to my room. It's the only thing that hasn't changed, and I like it that way. Promise me you won't do anything to my room."

Mom paused. "Dear heart, you look scared to death. Okay, I promise. We'll leave your room as it is until you decide to change it."

I smiled, relieved.

Dad would never believe all the changes in our house. If he ever came back, I hoped it wouldn't be at night. He'd stumble over his own TV chair just trying to get through the living room.

I had a feeling that if I could just get them together again, everything would work out. I was sure the trip to Disney World would do it.

Of course, I wasn't dumb enough to think Mom and I could casually bump into Dad on our way through the Magic Kingdom. It would take planning, but I had already figured it out.

I would get tickets for one of Dad's tours. What could they do then? In front of so many people they'd have to be civil. I thought of my dad that night in the limousine. How handsome he was as he showed me the sights! Next, I remembered when Dad was still working for TourMobile and he gave my third-grade class a free tour. He'd joked around with Miss Forsythe, our teacher. On a tour it wouldn't take long for Mom to be laughing along with Dad, smiling and blushing just like Miss Forsythe.

"So what are your plans tomorrow?" Dad would say to Mom.

"Stephanie won a trip to Disney World. Want to go along?"

It would be perfect. Mom would be dressed up, her hair brushed and shiny. She'd be relaxed, and since Mr. Delvechio was paying for everything, she wouldn't be worried about money.

Mostly, though, she'd be seeing Dad at his best. That night he'd take us around in his limousine.

I thought over all this as I sat at my desk and tore a piece of paper out of my spiral binder. Picking up a pencil, I wrote at the top of the paper in big letters, "PROJECT TIP TOP TOUR TEAM." Then I wrote down the things I would need to do:

1. Write to Sunshine Tours for tickets.
2. Make sure it's Dad's tour.
3. Keep tickets a secret from Mom and Dad.

I wasn't worried about paying for the tickets since I still had my birthday money tucked away in an envelope in my sock drawer. What I didn't bother to write down was the most important thing: None of this was possible unless I won the contest. But I knew I was going to win. I just had to.

For a long minute I could do no more than stare at PROJECT TTTT. So much to do. Sighing, I pulled out a piece of good stationery from the box Aunt Milly had given me at Christmas. Then I opened up my sock drawer and slid a crisp twenty-dollar bill out of an envelope.

March 3

Dear Sunshine Tour People,

    This is urgent.

    Please send me two tickets for a tour to Disney World in Reid Kulik's white limousine. The reason I want Reid Kulik is because I know he gives the best tours.

    I hope my $20 is enough.

    This is important. I am coming to Orlando next month.

    Thank you.

Sincerely,

Allison Lampe

"You did what?" Allison shrieked when I told her I'd signed her name to my letter.

We were on the phone. Since the phone is in the

kitchen, I had to wait until Mom had left her scraps of paper to do a load of laundry.

"I can't repeat it. My mom might hear."

"Great! What about my mom? What am I supposed to tell her when the tickets come from Florida?"

It really killed me how Allison thought she had problems. She should try switching with me.

"Tell her it's for geography class."

"Geography? Are you crazy? We had that last year. Honestly, Stephanie, my mom's never going to believe this!"

I drew boxes on a piece of paper. "Sure she is. Your mom is cool."

"I don't know, Stephie. If I wasn't your best friend . . . This whole thing is getting out of hand."

"But you said you would help me," I cried. "You don't have the slightest idea what it's like not having both a mom and a dad. Let me tell you. It's the end of the world. If I'd signed my name, my dad might find out. Don't you see? The surprise would be ruined. C'mon, Ali," I begged.

"Okay, okay."

The next morning I stopped on my way out the front door to look in the mirror, but Mom had moved it. All that was left was the nail hole.

I zipped up my jacket. I wasn't going to ask where she'd put the mirror. It was probably better this way. Now I wouldn't have to look at the angry zits about to explode on my forehead. I tugged on my bangs, hoping to cover them up.

It wasn't fair. Ever since Dad left, my whole body had gone berserk.

"Honey," Mom said, coming up behind me, "it's supposed to rain and it's cold outside. Let me drive you." She reached inside the closet for her coat.

"No, Mom. It's not cold. It's just breezy."

"We can pick up Allison on the way."

"No, Mom. We're riding the bus."

Worse than the way my mother is always moving the furniture around, worse even than zits, is how she babies me.

Life was too cruel.

Our school bus stop at the corner of Maple and Pine is the second to the last on the route. That means most of the time Allison and I can't even sit together because all the seats are already taken. But if Allison and I cut through the neighborhood, we can get on at Branch. Then we can usually sit together.

Today we decided it was crucial that we sit together. No way did I want to endure Mike Pierce without Allison for moral support.

We made it to Branch just in time.

I barely had my foot inside the door when Mike started squeaking from the back of the bus.

"Squeak, squeak." We could hear him all the way at the front.

"Ignore him," Allison said under her breath.

I whirled around and glared. "No way am I letting him get away with this."

"Squeak, squeak."

"You can stop your stupid squeaking, Michael Pierce!" I shouted. "You think you're so funny."

"No funnier than you, Kulik. Squeak. Squeak."

Apparently it was a planned attack. Everyone on the bus started to make squeaking noises. Even the dinky first graders were swinging their legs and squeaking.

"Hey, is there a chocolate mouse on the bus?" Michael hooted.

Everyone laughed, including the bus driver.

"Obviously I wouldn't recognize the sound," I said as I plopped down onto my seat. "I can only recognize a certain person being stupid and cruel as usual. Somebody ought to fumigate you off this bus, Michael Pierce," I hollered so everyone could hear.

"Cool it, Kulik."

"Oh, Stephanie," Deidra Carroll sang out. "You'll be happy to know they're serving grilled cheese sandwiches for lunch today. Nibble, nibble, yum, yum."

Everyone giggled, and my face started to burn.

I turned in my seat to give Mike my if-looks-could-kill glare. Ray Brown saw me first. He put his thumbs in his ears and waved his fingers. "Or maybe it's chocolate moooossse. *Mooooosssse*."

Beside me Allison tapped my shoulder. "Hang in

there. We're almost at school. Whatever you do, don't let them know you're angry or they'll never stop."

"That's easy for you to say, Ali," I whispered.

I was never so happy in my entire life as I was when the bus pulled up in the circular driveway and opened its doors. As all the others scrambled to grab their books and start down the aisle, I looked over my shoulder at Mike. I didn't care that he was smiling at me. I glared the meanest warning I could. Then I turned back around and stuck out my leg, hoping to trip him. But at the last minute he saw and jumped over.

"I wouldn't have minded if Michael Pierce had fallen flat on his fat face," I told Allison as we got off the bus. "He'd better not mess with me. And he'd better not win that contest."

"Honestly, I wish you wouldn't get so upset," Allison said.

"I'm going to get my parents back together, and nobody is going to stop me." I stomped up the steps and headed toward our classroom.

Behind me I heard Allison call out, but I didn't bother turning around. "Give me a break," she said. "I'm trying to be your friend."

I ducked my head as I headed into our classroom. Nobody understood. Nobody would ever understand. Without Dad, life was a big forehead full of zits.

Chapter 5

Chocolate Concoctions

"We have to think of something else for our ice cream," I told Allison one day on our way home from school.

For two weeks we'd been trying to invent the thirty-second flavor in Allison's kitchen, but so far nothing tasted quite right. The Peanut Brittle Battle tasted like gargle, the Popcorn Poppers Delight turned soggy, and the Bubble Gum Galore stuck to Allison's braces. We broke all our fingernails shelling pistachios for Pistachio Supreme de la Creme, and when we tried cutting up marshmallows for Marshmallow Mania, we ruined Mrs. Lampe's scissors.

Needless to say, Mrs. Lampe wasn't pleased about her scissors. How were we supposed to know we shouldn't melt the marshmallows first? The bag didn't say.

Meanwhile, Allison and I were developing a whole new appreciation for the culinary arts—and for ice cream in particular.

"It's really nice of your mom to buy all the ingredients." I wanted Allison to know how grateful I was.

"I know. I just wish she hadn't taken it personally when you asked her why she hadn't bought the grapes without seeds. You never should have done that, Steph. You shouldn't be so picky."

"I couldn't help it. I need to win this thing, and I can't do it without the right ingredients. It really kills me how you're not taking this contest seriously. Did you really think it was funny when you said we should call the flavor Red Grape Spittutti Frutti?"

I hadn't said it to be silly, but apparently Allison couldn't help it. She started to giggle. If she'd been laughing at anything besides this contest, I might have laughed too. For some reason I couldn't. Winning the contest meant everything to me.

"So far nothing is spectacular enough to come even close to first prize," I said glumly.

Allison shrugged. "What about that Peppermint Banana Peanut Butter Fudge Nut Royale? That was pretty spectacular."

"Boring. All that stuff made it about as thrilling as a two-day-old cold casserole. What we need is something absolutely out of the ordinary." I shook my head. "Instead of relying on your mom, this time let's go to the store ourselves."

Later that afternoon, after Allison had finished cleaning up her room while I helped Mrs. Lampe with

Matthew, we finally got to the store. It was like being on a treasure hunt for a rare, exotic, and secret jewel. All we needed was that perfect missing ingredient, which no one else—particularly pesky Mike Pierce—would know.

I grabbed a cart outside the Safeway and led the way up and down the aisles past the other shoppers. The whole time we scanned the shelves, searching.

"Wait a second. We might need some extra chocolate," I said, eyeing the Hershey's display at the end of the next aisle. I dropped a brown plastic squeeze bottle in the cart and continued on. Halfway down the next aisle I stopped.

"Allison, I can't believe it. Look at that sign! This is perfect!"

A purple sign with fancy white letters told us we were in exactly the right place:

Very Special Foods
Gourmet & International Specialties

On both sides of the aisle were foods I'd never seen before.

"You know"—Allison glanced around—"I must have been in this store at least a million times with my mother, and I don't remember ever seeing this."

"Me neither," I said. "Maybe it's new."

Allison whistled. "Probably it's the prices. Ex-*pen*-sive." She pointed to the top shelf. "What's that red stuff? That would at least *look* pretty. I mean, if we can afford it. See, it's up there."

I craned my neck. "Red peppers. I don't think so, Ali."

"Nope. It would probably melt our ice cream faster than the microwave."

"What about that box of chocolate mousse?" I said, careful to pronounce the word correctly. "It looks like a plain old box of pudding mix to me, but it's got to be better than that or it wouldn't be over here in Very Special Foods." I stood on the base of the cart and stretched to reach.

"Ooooooh, what's this?" Allison held up a glass jar. "Pickled okra. Oooh, don't they look like green fingers?" She held them out for me to see. "Hey, wouldn't these be great for a haunted house on Halloween? Anybody would believe they were gangrened fingers. I bet nobody uses pickled okra for the thirty-second flavor."

"Right. Including me." Meanwhile, I noticed the cans of U.S. Senate bean soup. Not that I'd want to put beans in ice cream either, but the picture of the Capitol on the can reminded me of my New Year's Eve date with Dad. The Capitol had been so pretty and sparkly at night.

"It says this pickled okra is the talk of Texas," Allison said, still reading the label. "I should think so. It doesn't say anything about being microwavable. Remember what happened with the marshmallows?

Of course, we'd never cut these gory little fingers with scissors. We'd use a knife."

"Give me that." I yanked the jar out of Allison's hand and put it back on the shelf.

That's when I saw the perfect missing ingredient. Original wild Swedish lingonberries in sugar. They were in a squat glass jar with a white screw-top lid.

"Allison, what's a lingonberry?"

"A fruit, I guess. I wonder if they're good." She cocked her head, thinking. "In my whole life I don't think I've ever had a Swedish lingonberry. Maybe I had an American lingonberry when we went camping, but I don't remember."

I picked up the jar and turned it over in my hand. "Listen to what it says on the label. 'Lingonberries have a delicious flavor, combining sweetness and tartness. They have ripened in the intense summer of northern Sweden, where the summer sun never sets.'"

"Wow." Allison blinked. "Where the summer sun never sets." She sighed.

"I know," I said. "It sounds so good."

"What else does it say?"

" 'Serve with meat, game, and poultry.'"

"Oh."

" 'On pancakes, rolls, and toast,'" I continued. Then I practically screamed with joy. I could hardly believe my luck! " 'Or as an ice-cream topping'!"

"Wow! Perfect!" Allison's eyes grew as big as dinner plates. "You are definitely going to win. Nobody would ever think of Swedish lingonberries. How much are they?"

"Four dollars and sixty-nine cents."

"Yikes! For that little jar?"

"Doesn't matter. It's my birthday money. Besides, it's for my father, and he's definitely worth it."

I laid the jar of lingonberries gently in the cart beside the Hershey's syrup.

Suddenly Allison screamed. "Oh, no! It's Mike Pierce!"

She jumped on the cart as if it were a sled, hiding everything. She was holding on to the sides for dear life with her legs sticking straight out like two battering rams.

I grabbed the cart and started running as fast as I could to get away from Mike Pierce. But with Allison on top, the cart wouldn't go the way I wanted. It kept lurching to one side or the other.

"Keep your legs still," I shouted to Allison. "I can't steer."

"I'll fall off," she yelled back.

"No, you won't! Hold on. We've got to make it to the checkout."

At the end of the aisle I made a sharp turn, narrowly missing the eggs. I ran down the next aisle and rounded the corner to make a wide turn, heading directly for the checkout. That was when Allison's legs snagged the kosher foods display. Matzoh balls, potato kugel mix, and Sabbath candles fell all over the place.

Talk about humiliation.

When Allison slid off the cart, I tossed my jacket into it. Only the plastic squeeze bottle of Hershey's chocolate showed.

"So what are you doing here?" said Mike's familiar voice.

"Same thing you are, Michael Pierce." I glared at him.

"Buying toothpicks and toilet paper?" he said, not missing a beat. "I don't see that in your cart."

Just as I expected, he was eyeing our cart.

"Ha!" he snickered. "Don't tell me you expect to win Mr. Delvechio's contest with something as amateurish as chocolate."

"And don't tell me you expect to win Mr. Delvechio's contest just because you always win everything," I said right back.

Recovered from her wild ride, Allison stepped forward. "Why don't you do us a big favor and dis—"

She never had a chance to finish. Just then the loudspeaker crackled and a voice announced, "Cleanup in aisle seven. Cleanup in aisle seven."

Michael Pierce cracked up.

"That's your mess they're talking about. Nice work, Kulik. You single-handedly canceled Passover."

Life, I was coming to understand, was not fair.

Back at Allison's we didn't waste any time—mainly because both of us were dying of starvation and curiosity. Mrs. Lampe was in the family room watching her favorite soap opera, and Matthew was napping. That meant we'd have at least a half hour without any interruptions.

Quickly we assembled a bowl and a spoon, a couple of scoops of Mr. Delvechio's vanilla, the chocolate syrup, and, of course, the jar of original wild Swedish lingonberries.

"Here, you stir." I slid the bowl of ice cream toward Allison. "And don't eat any," I ordered as I excitedly squirted bursts of chocolate syrup into the mixture.

"Be careful!" Allison cried. "You're splattering chocolate on my shirt. Yours too."

"Sorry." I opened a drawer and rummaged for a spoon. I was already beginning to imagine the taste of lingonberries with chocolate.

As I plopped the thick lingonberry sauce into the ice cream, Allison stirred it into a bright purple swirl. Here and there plump, delicious lingonberries peeked through a light brown cream. Mmm.

"Hey, this looks pretty good," Allison said.

"Smells good, too," I said as I placed it in the freezer and set the timer.

While we stared at the refrigerator, waiting for the ding, Allison said, "Remember when your father used to take us to the mall? It was fun the way he let us hog the glass elevators, riding up and down, up and down."

"Stopping at every level!" I could feel a smile spread across my face. "The best was running up the down escalators in Neiman Marcus."

"I never told my folks," Allison whispered. "There's probably a law against it."

"Remember that snooty old lady in the fur coat who gave us that horrified look? She had purple eyes and runny red lips."

"Dah-ling." Allison minced around the kitchen, pretending to swoop a fur over her shoulder. "It was fun with your father," she said. "When do you think the tickets will come from Sunshine Tours? Are you sure you sent them to the right address?"

"Yes. I must have checked a million times."

Allison was quiet. "What do you think your father's up to in Florida?" she said after a minute. "I mean, while he gets ready for your Tip Top Tour Team? You still haven't heard from him, have you? If it was my father, he would have at least called."

"No," I said as lightly as I could, trying to ignore the comparison with Allison's dad. "He's probably showing people around in Florida. Maybe he's feeding the dolphins."

"He's probably lying around on a beach staring up at the sun," Allison said right back.

"No, giving tours is what he does best. That's what he's doing."

"I don't know." Allison shook her head. "I didn't think your father *liked* working. I thought that's what all the fighting was about."

"I don't know what you're talking about," I said,

trying to disguise the quiver in my voice. "There wasn't any fighting."

"Yes, there was. I heard them. Remember when I was spending the night? It was scary. I thought we should call 9-1-1, but you said that they screamed like that all the time."

"I never said that."

"Did too."

"Well." I shrugged my shoulders. "Anyway, if I could just get them together again. That's why the contest is so perfect. Everything will be better when we get to Disney World. It'll be cotton candy and one ride after another."

In my mind I kept picturing the ride that shows up in all the magazines: Dumbo hanging from wires like one of those kiddie airplane rides in all the carnivals. Only Dumbo is bigger, of course, and looks like a lot more fun. I picture his ears flapping up and down. I am in the front seat, looking out over Dumbo's hat. My mom and dad are in the seat behind me. Their laughter floats through the air.

Just then the timer dinged.

My throat hurt more than I could ever say.

A few minutes later we were leaning against the counter, our eyes closed as we concentrated on the taste.

"What do you think?"

"I don't know," Allison answered. "What do you think?"

"Kind of sweet. Kind of sour. Maybe more sour than sweet. You think it's too sour?"

There was a long pause before Allison said cautiously, "Maybe it's the chocolate."

I dropped my spoon, I was so startled. "What do you mean, maybe it's the chocolate?"

"I mean, maybe it's not chocolate enough."

I really had to hand it to Allison. "Brilliant! Chocolate is always the perfect solution. Tomorrow we'll add gobs more chocolate!"

Allison rolled her eyes and muttered under her breath.

Since my mom has a late class every Tuesday night, I stay and eat dinner with the Lampes. Before my dad left, I always felt comfortable sitting at the table with Mr. Lampe, but now I felt a little shy. Whenever I looked at him—say he was passing me the ketchup or something—I'd have to look away real quick so he wouldn't see my eyes filling up with tears. I couldn't help it. I kept thinking how nice it would be if Mom, Dad, and I could be a normal family like the Lampes.

I also thought that if Dad didn't know what it took to be a good husband, I could tell him by observing Mr. Lampe. I had already noticed how when Mr. Lampe came home from work, the first thing he did was kiss Mrs. Lampe on the cheek. Then he might pick Matthew up and swing him in the air or tap

Allison on the shoulder and give her a hug. Once when they didn't know I was watching, I saw Mrs. Lampe give Mr. Lampe a tap on his backside. I thought it would be nice when I had that kind of family. I would, as soon as I won the trip to Disney World.

This particular Tuesday was St. Patrick's Day so Mrs. Lampe had tinted scrambled eggs with green food coloring and served green eggs and ham. It was great fun. We were still at the kitchen table with Matthew in his high chair when the doorbell rang.

Mr. Lampe stood up. "I'll get it. Honey, it's Rosemary," he hollered a few minutes later.

I glanced at Allison. Rosemary was Mike's mom.

If you want to know the truth, Mrs. Pierce isn't nearly as good-looking as her son. She's rounder. Much rounder. Probably from testing all the delicious foods she makes for her catering business, Pierce's Perfections.

Before I knew what was happening, Mr. Lampe whisked Matthew into the bathroom to clean the green eggs off his face and hands. Meanwhile, we could hear Mrs. Lampe and Mrs. Pierce chattering away as they headed toward the kitchen.

"I'm sorry. I didn't mean to interrupt your meal," Mrs. Lampe was saying. "But if you have some cinnamon, it would save a trip to the store."

"No problem. We just finished eating."

Allison and I do have good manners. When Mrs.

Lampe said that we had just finished eating, we knew to get up and begin clearing the table.

"Come on in the kitchen. I'm sure I have some cinnamon." Mrs. Lampe stopped when she saw us carrying dishes to the sink. "Well, on second thought, maybe I don't. The girls have been doing extra duty in the cooking department. Lately I seem to run out of all sorts of things."

"Oh." Mrs. Pierce's eyes got as big as the dinner plate I held in my hand. "Are you girls involved in that contest too?"

"Involved!" Mrs. Lampe laughed. "These girls live, eat, and breathe ice cream. Peanut brittle, gone! Raisins, gone! Marshmallows, gone!" She shook her head. "I'm at the store every day replacing what they used the afternoon before."

"It's the same at my house!" Mrs. Pierce almost shouted. "With Michael it's my super sorbet maker. He runs it nonstop!"

"And the chocolate practically evaporates," Mrs. Lampe went on. "Chocolate syrup, chocolate chips, chocolate candy . . ."

I couldn't believe what I was hearing. Right in front of us, Mrs. Lampe was revealing our secrets to the enemy.

Allison kept shaking her head at her mother, but apparently Mrs. Lampe didn't recognize the signal because she went right on blabbing away. Finally Allison yelled, "Mother, stop! Look who you're telling.

Mike's going to know everything we're doing. It's a contest! What we're doing is a secret. You're not supposed to tell."

Mrs. Lampe blushed. "Oops. I didn't realize . . . I'm sure Mrs. Pierce won't say anything."

"No, of course not," Mrs. Pierce reassured us. "Although I have to say my Michael is dying to know what you girls are up to. Of course, I can't imagine why it would matter. His flavors are so good I'm tempted to use them for my catering events. Michael's only problem is the decision process. All his flavors are so delicious he can't seem to make up his mind which recipe to submit. He must have at least a hundred different flavors to choose from."

I couldn't help myself. "A hundred?" I stammered. Allison and I had exactly none.

Still looking embarrassed about her mistake, Mrs. Lampe put her hand gently on my shoulder. "Girls, why don't you go on upstairs? You spent all afternoon making ice cream, which means you haven't had time to do your homework. Don't worry about the dishes. I'll take care of everything."

"I'm sorry about my mom's loose lips," Allison whispered as we headed toward the stairs.

"Don't worry about it." But to tell the truth, I wasn't exactly grateful to Mrs. Lampe for spilling the beans to Mrs. Pierce. And I wasn't exactly comfortable knowing that Mike had more than a hundred delicious flavors and that his biggest problem was deciding which one was the best. I was sure Mike had sent his mother to spy on us. As far as I was concerned, he left us no choice. Somehow Allison and I would have to find out what flavors Mike had concocted for the contest.

Chapter 6

A Million
and One Flavors

"No! Not ice cream again!" Allison and I were arguing about what we were going to do that afternoon. "We never do anything else," Allison shrieked loud enough to wake Matthew from his nap. "We haven't ridden our bikes since the last century."

Sometimes Allison can be so dramatic. Her mother blames it on preadolescence, but I don't believe that for a minute. After all, Allison and I are the same age and you don't see me throwing fits.

"Shh! You woke up Matthew." I took the jar of original wild Swedish lingonberries out of the refrigerator and set it on the counter. "Besides, you can't ride bikes through snow."

Allison tossed her hair, acting more like Deidra than I cared to admit. "It's not snowing now." She put one hand on her hip and pointed out the window with the other. "See that? In case you don't recognize it, Steph, that is the sun! The same sun that never sets over lingonberries. And if we don't get out of the kitchen once in a while and start doing something else, we'll be as exciting to be around as dirty dishrags."

"Girls, girls!" Mrs. Lampe stood in the doorway, toting Matthew on her hip. He obviously wasn't feeling well. His nose was running, and he kept rubbing his eyes with his tight little fist. When I walked over to him, instead of holding his arms out to me the way he usually did, he turned away and buried his face in his mother's neck.

"What's the matter with Matthew?" I asked.

"He has a cold, I'm afraid." Mrs. Lampe tried to untangle his fist from her hair, but then Matthew reared back in her arms while still holding on with his sticky little fingers. Ouch! I bet that hurt.

"I was hoping you girls wouldn't mind doing a favor for me. I'd do it, but then I'd have to ask you girls to watch Matthew, and right now he's awfully grouchy."

Allison rolled her eyes and groaned.

"Sure, Mrs. Lampe," I said, trying to stop an argument before it started. "Do you want us to go to the store again? I really wanted to get some more ingredients for the contest. We could ride our bikes. Right, Allison?"

Allison gave me another weird look. I knew what she was thinking. I'd ride bikes only if it involved ice cream.

"No, not the store. Rosemary—" Mrs. Lampe

corrected herself. "Mrs. Pierce has a catering job this afternoon, and she took Mike along with her. There's no one at their house to let their dog out, and Mrs. Pierce bought a nice new carpet only last week. I told her last night on the phone that I could do it, but now that Matthew isn't feeling well . . ." Mrs. Lampe raised her eyebrows expectantly at Allison. "Rosemary dropped her key off this morning. It would be a shame if . . ."

Allison raised her shoulders and let out a long, painful breath. "Mom, do we look like dog-letter-outers?"

"No, darling. I wouldn't mind driving over to Rosemary's and being a dog-letter-outer myself if you and Stephanie would take care of Matthew."

Allison gave Matthew's drippy nose a sidelong glance. "Yuck!"

But even as Allison argued with her mother, I began to see the possibilities. If Allison and I were alone at Mike's house, we could check out his secret flavors. Maybe that wasn't such a nice thing to do, but since his mother had come snooping around at Allison's, why couldn't we spy at Mike's house?

"No problem, Mrs. Lampe," I said brightly. "What Allison means is that we wanted to go bike riding. But we could still do that. We'll be glad to ride over to Mike's house and let Poochie out."

I gave Allison a sidelong glance and winked, trying to communicate what I had in mind. When

Mrs. Lampe reached around the corner for a Kleenex to wipe Matthew's nose, I put my hand up to my mouth and whispered frantically to Allison, so there would be no doubt, "Do you believe it? This is perfect. Now we can check out Mike's flavors."

Allison's eyes lit up. "Sure, Mom," she said, "you stay home and take good care of Matthew. Stephanie and I will go over to the Pierces'. We'll wipe our feet before we go in and lock the door behind us when we leave."

"And you'll make sure Poochie does her stuff in the yard?"

"Don't worry, Mrs. Lampe. Everything is under control. We'll give Poochie the Wonder Dog a good workout in the backyard. Won't we, Allison?"

"Yep." Allison grinned.

If Mrs. Lampe was puzzled by Allison's change of heart, she didn't show it. She was too busy rocking Matthew in her arms while rubbing his bottom. "What would I do without you girls?" she said softly. She turned slightly so I could see Matthew's face. "Is he sleeping?"

"Almost," I whispered. "He's so sweet."

"Except when he has a cold." She nodded toward the family room. "Mrs. Pierce's keys are on the hall table. Are you girls sure you feel comfortable about going into that big house when no one's home?"

"We don't mind a bit. We'll be fine, won't we, Allison?"

"Fine, Mom," Allison repeated.

We had to fight hard not to let our silly grins betray us.

A few minutes later we were parking our bikes near the rhododendron bushes beside Mike's driveway.

"Good deal," I muttered. "Nobody's here but us."

Allison turned the key in the lock. "Yeah, just the two of us and Mike's one hundred and one delicious flavors."

"Don't forget about Poochie."

What a silly thing to say. We could hear Poochie yapping on the other side of the door.

I'd never been inside Mike Pierce's house before. It wasn't anything like ours. For one thing, it was a lot cleaner. For another, the marble foyer was at least as big as our kitchen.

Allison shut the door behind us with a loud click. Hearing it, Poochie scrambled away from us, sliding across the slick marble. She sat underneath the chandelier and started barking her poodle head off.

Feeling sorry for Poochie, who was obviously frightened by us, I got down on my knees. "Here, Poochie. Nice puppy." I held my hand out and bent my face down so she could lick my cheek with her strawberry tongue.

Meanwhile, Allison strode straight down the hallway toward what we hoped was the kitchen.

"Hey, Ali, wait up!" I called. "Don't forget about Poochie." For someone who placed such a high priority on originality, I would have thought Mike and his family could have come up with a better name for the white ball of fluff that darted around my legs as I hurried after Allison. "Come on, let's get . . ." I started to say when Allison suddenly hollered.

"Omigosh! It's Mike."

I whirled. "Where?"

Allison pointed. "On the wall. That picture. I'd recognize Mike Pierce anywhere."

I'd seen huge family portraits hanging in people's hallways before, and wedding pictures where everyone is smiling about a lifetime of bliss. I had even seen First Communion portraits of saintly little girls in white veils with white rosary beads draped over their praying hands. But I had never seen a baby picture of someone I knew blown up this big and hanging in a public place.

It was Michael Pierce all right.

Mike was sitting in the middle of a red-and-white-checkered picnic blanket. He had shiny blond hair cut in bangs and a big smile on his face. He was holding a chocolate ice cream cone that was dribbling down his chin and chubby little tummy. It took a couple of seconds before something else sank in. Mike was sitting on that blanket naked.

"It's a good thing his mother put that teddy bear in the picture," I whispered to Allison.

"How embarrassing!" Allison giggled. "Mike Pierce in the raw."

We couldn't help ourselves. We edged closer to the

biggest picture I'd ever seen in my life of a naked baby. And to think it was Mike.

"Isn't he too adorable?" Allison said after a few minutes of staring.

I didn't know what to say. How could you call the boy who antagonized you every minute of every day adorable, especially when he wasn't wearing even a single stitch?

I chuckled under my breath. "Wouldn't Mike just die if he knew we were ogling his picture."

Just then Poochie started to whine. Suddenly she darted toward the living room.

"Quick!" I yelled. "Poochie's headed for the Persian carpet!"

You would have thought Allison was on her way to scoring the winning touchdown instead of saving Mrs. Pierce's carpet from a Poochie puddle. She scooped Poochie off the floor and raced down the hallway toward some sliding glass doors in the kitchen. Following more slowly, I watched Allison set Poochie down on the patio and walk toward the grass, beckoning the little dog to follow.

After a few minutes I turned back to the kitchen and what we had really come for.

Mrs. Pierce's freezer was silver and wide with two long doors, like a double closet. I guessed Mrs. Pierce needed a super deluxe model because she was in the catering business. The only time I'd ever seen anything like it was on a quiz show. For a moment I wasn't sure which of the two silver doors to try first. I picked the one on the left and gave it a hard yank.

"Yaaah!" I jumped back thinking I'd seen a snake. A closer look showed me that Mike had curled pieces of licorice around the freezer shelf to look like a snake. I was glad Mike hadn't seen me. My reaction was exactly what he wanted.

"Mike Pierce is definitely weird!"

Carefully I shifted containers around in the freezer. Mrs. Pierce had more Tupperware than a Tupperware factory. She even had matching lids—something I didn't see much at home.

"Whatever he's made, it should be in small—" I stopped speaking as I saw stacks and stacks of Styrofoam cups, all neatly capped with plastic and labeled with blue letters and numbers.

"Poochie did her business!" Allison hollered as she came inside. "I guess it's safe to let her inside." I heard her take a dog treat out of the box Mrs. Pierce had left on the counter.

"Good, 'cause you're not going to believe this unless you see it."

Allison joined me at the freezer and pulled a clipboard wrapped in plastic off a freezer shelf. Under the plastic were a computer printout and a pencil on a long stiff string.

"What is this?" Allison asked. "Mike keeps his homework in the freezer?"

"No, not his homework," I said. "He's even

stranger than we thought. It's his contest data . . . in code." It was almost as though Mike expected us to snoop.

Allison flipped over a page. "Hey! Mike's using his computer to invent flavors. The letters and numbers must stand for ingredients."

My eyes scanned the list, substituting ingredients for abbreviations in the code. "Chocolate peanut brittle one and chocolate peanut brittle two," I whooped. "We invented those flavors, the rat."

As angry as I was, I felt smug proving to Allison that what I'd suspected was true. Mike was spying on us and stealing our flavors. At the same time I felt defeated. I'd known it would be difficult trying to beat Mike with his mother's special cookbooks and machines. Now he was using his computer! If I weren't doing this for my father, I could easily have given up.

"Wait a minute," Allison was saying. "I wonder what's in the rest of their refrigerator."

"Gosh, Allison," I said, "make yourself at home." Then she opened the door on the right and gasped.

"Wow! Pierce's Perfections!"

We stood there, our mouths hanging as wide open as the door. We may have even drooled on Mrs. Pierce's tiled floor. Inside were the most stupendous desserts you could ever imagine. Towering whipped cream delights. Cherries and chocolate sprinkles on everything. Between the desserts were trays of tiny sandwiches, wrapped in Saran wrap, with little yellow notes that read DO NOT TOUCH! There were platters of sliced meats marked DO NOT TOUCH! as well. Everyone's mom left notes outside the refrigerator. But Mike's was the first I'd known to leave notes inside.

I sighed and closed the door. "Can you imagine coming home from school to that!" I said. I'd always had a mental picture of Mike sitting down to after-school banquets courtesy of Pierce's Perfections.

"Forget it," Allison interrupted. "You saw all those notes. How would you like not being allowed to touch anything in your own refrigerator? Poor Mike."

Allison's response surprised me. For a minute it almost sounded as though she actually felt sorry for Mike. When she blushed, I was sure of it. Was Allison beginning to like Mike? I'd have to watch her more closely from now on.

Thinking such a thing made my eyes water. Best friends, like families, were supposed to stick together.

When Allison whispered "Poor Mike" again, I pretended not to hear.

Chapter 7

One Lousy Postcard

I almost didn't see the postcard. Because of a brown and sticky substance on the stamp that bore an amazing resemblance to a chocolate-coated thumb-print, the postcard attached itself to a sales flyer. My mom almost threw it in the trash. It was pure luck that we saw the postcard at all.

The picture was of a man whacking a golf ball. "Hilton Head Heaven: A place where emerald green fairways stretch into dazzling blue skies" read the tiny print on the bottom of the card. Beside the brown sticky spot, the postmark read, "Hilton Head, South Carolina," with the date stamped in the middle.

I swallowed hard. No one in our house, my father included, played golf. And what was he doing in South Carolina when he was supposed to be in Florida? I held on to the card with shaking hands. The message was scrawled in blue ballpoint.

Stephanie—

How's my girl?

The weather here, like everything else, is beautiful. Tell your mother the money is on the way. I miss you.

Dad

"Tell your mother the money is on the way," I said under my breath. What money? Suddenly I knew.

"Money for our plane trip?" I almost shouted with glee. Just as I'd hoped, Dad had come through. No more worries about beating Mike and his 101 flavors of ice cream. "Is that what Dad means? Are we going to Disney—" Catching myself, I glanced down at the postcard. "I mean, are we going to Hilton Head? When? What's there? Is there an amusement park? Can I tell Allison?"

I couldn't help myself. There was so much I needed to know that the questions tumbled out of my mouth before I was aware of the tense expression on my mother's face.

"We're not going anywhere," she said, taking the postcard from me. "Your father has a responsibility to support you. The money he's talking about is for your food and clothes. He's supposed to help with our expenses, and he hasn't sent a dime."

"Oh. Where exactly is Hilton Head?"

"About halfway between here and Orlando."

"So it's north of Florida?" I started dancing around

the room with one of Mom's pillows. "Yippee! He's on his way home!"

Maybe I was acting childish and too silly for words, but just then Mom grabbed me by the shoulders. "Stephanie, get a grip. Look at the postmark," she said, sounding angry. "Two days ago. Don't you think that if your father *were* on his way here, he'd have already arrived? Wouldn't he have said, 'Tell Mom *I'm* on the way,' or, 'See you soon'?"

I let the pillow drop to the floor. Nothing made any sense.

"Maybe he never got to Orlando," I said slowly. "Maybe the car broke down."

"You mean his wonderful limousine?"

I tried hard to ignore the cutting sarcasm in Mom's voice, the nastiness that had never been there before.

"Yeah." My lips quivered. "It could have broken down. The windows didn't work so good. Neither did the heater. That's why he said the limo was perfect for Florida. The limousine wasn't new, you know," I said weakly. "It just *looked* new."

Mom picked up the pillow and flung it at the couch. That was what I thought she might have done to Dad if he'd been there. For his sake I was almost glad he wasn't.

"I don't know, Stephanie. But I can tell you one thing for sure: If your father had a problem on the highway and needed work done on his limousine, he wouldn't have thought twice about calling us. He made it to Orlando all right. He may have even taken that job he told you about."

I gulped. "Then what's he doing in Hilton Head?"

Mom collapsed on the couch and covered her eyes with her arm. "Sweetie, Hilton Head is a posh resort where very rich people play. I have no idea what your father is doing there or how long he intends to stay. I can only guess, and right now I'm not in the mood."

"Are you saying that we don't know where Dad is? Mom, this is a mess." When I reached for it, the postcard slipped through Mom's fingers as easily as a shadow. "What if we needed him?" I said. "What if something happened to you? Or to me? How would Dad know? You didn't even look surprised when you saw that the postcard wasn't from Florida. It's like you don't even care."

I must have struck a nerve. Mom sat up and looked me straight in the eye.

"Of course I care. It's just that I suspected something like this over a month ago when Mr. VanderCamp sent your father a certified letter. It was returned as undeliverable."

"Over a month ago?" I couldn't believe it. "Who's Mr. VanderCamp?"

Mom groaned. "I didn't want you to know all this just yet. Mr. VanderCamp is my lawyer."

"Your lawyer!" I shrieked. "What do you need a lawyer for?"

"When your father left, there was paperwork to be taken care of." Mom stood up and started to pace.

"I suppose I should call Mr. VanderCamp tomorrow," she said more to herself than to me. "I wonder when Reid got to South Carolina. I wonder how long he'll be there."

"Wait a minute, Mom." I reached out and grabbed her arm to stop her pacing. "If you knew Dad wasn't in Florida, how come you let me keep writing him those letters? You probably thought it was really dumb of me to write to someone who wasn't even there. How could you do that? You're supposed to be my mother. I'll bet you were laughing the whole time."

Mom was obviously startled by what I'd said. "Oh, no, darling. I could never laugh at you. It's just that in February you wouldn't have believed me. You weren't ready to listen, and I wasn't ready to snatch away your dreams. And according to Mr. VanderCamp, it's still entirely possible your letters are being forwarded to your father's new address, wherever that is. It could be that he just doesn't want me to know his address."

"That doesn't sound very responsible," I said.

"No, it doesn't."

I stared at Mom's back, slumped by the weight of one postcard, as she headed toward the kitchen.

In a way I knew how she felt.

I'd written Dad practically every day, and all I got in return were three sentences and a question on the back of a lousy postcard. I stomped up the stairs. One sentence wasn't even meant for me, but for my mother. Another sentence was about the weather! The question I couldn't even answer, since I didn't have his address. That meant there was one sentence left. Can you believe it? In three months I got one lousy sentence on a postcard of a dumb golfer.

He missed me. Who was he kidding? I slammed my bedroom door behind me so hard the house rattled.

I was mad at Dad, sure, but I was mad at Mom, too. She should have told me Dad wasn't in Florida. I wasn't some dumb kid. She should have had more respect. She should have let me know.

Angrily I ripped the postcard to shreds and let the pieces drop to the floor. Then I threw myself on my bed and cried until I thought my heart would break.

"I miss you."

For three months I had wanted to believe that was true.

I had wanted to believe he was thinking of me as much as I thought about him. But then why had he left like that, and why hadn't I heard from him? If he wasn't going to be in Florida, why didn't he call? Was that so much to ask?

If he wasn't in Disney World, what about the contest? I had spent almost all my birthday money trying to get Mom and me to Disney World, and now he wasn't even there! What was Dad thinking of? Certainly not me!

Then, as I blew my nose, something occurred to me. Maybe Dad had left Florida on a short vacation. If he was working really hard showing the tourists all the sights, he might need a break. Maybe he was going back to Disney World and Mom and I could still surprise him there. Maybe there was still hope. Maybe I could still get my parents back together again. I couldn't help thinking about what Allison heard my mother say to her mom: "If I could just talk to Reid."

Just because Mom was mad at Dad now didn't mean she had to be mad at him forever. Didn't I always forgive him? Why couldn't she be more like me? If I could find him, if I could get all of us together in Disney World, maybe there could be some small glimmer of hope after all.

Then it hit me. What was stopping me from calling the one place that would be able to locate Reid Kulik? Just because they hadn't answered my letter didn't mean I couldn't call Sunshine Tours.

I glanced at the clock. Five-fifteen. Sunshine Tours might still be open. I would get the number from the long-distance operator.

With Mom in the kitchen (probably rearranging her pots and pans) there was no problem using the phone. Still, I tiptoed into Mom's bedroom and whispered into the receiver. What I was doing felt very sneaky. Mom had enough trouble paying the bills without my racking up more with long-distance phone calls. But then I reasoned that the bill wouldn't come for at least another month. If everything went the way I planned, Mom and Dad would be back together by then. In a month's time they could be sitting on the couch, laughing over the phone bill together.

"What city are you calling?"

"Orlando," I told the operator.

"Orlando speaking. Go ahead."

"Would you please connect me with Sunshine Tours?"

"One moment."

The connection was so clear I could have been dialing Allison instead of another state. It rang several times before a woman finally answered. I told her what I wanted, and although I hadn't meant to, I told her why. I even told her Allison hadn't written that letter asking for a Reid Kulik tour. There was a long silence. Then came the really sad part.

"Honey, I'm sorry, but we haven't seen your father since I can't tell you when. We're holding a stack of mail for him."

I hung up as quickly as I could and hurried back to my room. Sniffing, I turned the radio on as loud as I could, hoping my mother would scream at me to turn it down so I could scream back. When she didn't, I lay across the bed on my stomach, sobbing into my pillow.

There ought to be a law against parents who let their kids down. There ought to be a judge somewhere who rounds up all the lousy parents, throws them in a lousy jail, and throws away the lousy key. If I wanted to be truthful with myself, I could probably have fallen asleep counting the times my father had let me down. But who wanted to count that high? Besides, what would it accomplish? As far as I knew, there was no such judge and no such jail. Parents could go on disappointing their kids just because they had nothing better to do.

It wasn't fair.

No one wants to think bad things about her parents. But now I couldn't deny it any longer.

I must have fallen asleep. The next thing I knew my room was black as night and my mom was tapping on my bedroom door.

"May I come in?"

I sat up cross-legged on my bed and rubbed my eyes. "Sure."

Mom balanced a tray in one hand as she flipped on the wall switch. "Will soup and a cheese sandwich be enough for dinner? I didn't have the energy for much else."

"That's fine. Thanks." I leaned back against the wall, allowing Mom to set the tray in my lap. "Remember when I was little and had a sore throat? You used to prop me up with pillows and feed me goldfish soup."

Mom laughed. "It wasn't really goldfish."

"I thought it was."

"Chicken noodle with goldfish crackers."

"It always made me feel better."

Mom pushed my hair gently off my forehead. "If only I had goldfish crackers now, sweetie. It would make us both feel better."

I nodded and stirred the noodles absently while Mom picked the remains of the postcard off the floor.

"Mom," I said, my voice shaking, "I called Dad a little while ago. It was long distance. If you want, I'll pay for it out of the money Aunt Milly gave me for my birthday." I didn't tell Mom that I hoped it wouldn't be too much. My savings had dwindled considerably from buying ingredients for the ice-cream contest.

"I don't mind paying, Stephanie. You should be able to call your father whenever you want."

"But, Mom, he wasn't there. You were right. The lady at Sunshine Tours said he hasn't been there for a long, long time. I guess you'll have to tell Mr. VanderCamp that."

Mom tickled my toes lightly with her fingers. "I'm sorry, sweetie. I tried to protect you. I can see now that there was no way I could keep you from getting hurt."

"Yeah." I sniffed. "That's the thing, Mom. There are lots of kids in school whose parents are divorced. It's not like I never heard of the word. It's just different when it happens to you." I was trying to think what it was like. "It's worse than when my hamster died."

As awful as I felt, I didn't have the energy to call

Allison. Getting the postcard and finding out my dad wasn't where he'd said he'd be weren't things I wanted to talk about—not even to my best friend.

I went to sleep thinking that when my father left, at least I'd had someone to write to. Then I'd had a reason to want to win Mr. Delvechio's ice-cream contest. Now I had nothing. No father, no one to write to, and not one good reason for wanting to win a trip to Disney World. Thanks to my father, I didn't even have a dream.

Chapter 8

Down the Drain

There are times when you sit inside a car and everything on the other side of the window looks pretty interesting. There are other times when everything seems pretty dumb. The next morning, as my mother drove me to school because we'd both overslept, was one of those dumb times.

I guess she was feeling the same. She didn't feel like talking, and that was okay by me. We both sat there like zombies as the car moved through traffic. If we had been going in circles, I don't think either one of us would have noticed.

What I did notice was that she hadn't gotten any more sleep than I had. Except for the purple shadows under her eyes, she could have passed for a ghost. Since I hadn't found her books in the kitchen when I got up, I knew she wasn't tired from studying. It was something else. I could guess what that something else was.

I had to force myself not to think about my father.

By the time I got to school, my teacher was doing math problems on the chalkboard. I shuffled into class and plopped my attendance card on her desk. When she nodded in my direction, I slid into my seat and scrunched up as small as possible.

Allison's note, folded up like a football, appeared on my desk during history. Being careful that no one could see, I bent over my desk and carefully unfolded it.

Any other day Allison's cheery little missive would have made me delirious with joy. Not today. Not for the rest of my whole depressing life.

Steph—
Where were you last night? I left a message on your machine. How come you didn't call me back? What do you think of these new flavors? Can't wait to try them. Yum. Yum.

Celery Surprise
Carrot Stick Chip
Peanut Butter Bongo
Bongo Bongo Berries
Lingonbongo Cheesecake

What do you say we test all five flavors today? Get psyched. We've got to catch up with Mike.

Ali

I wanted to cry, but I didn't. Instead I scrawled a quick note back to Allison saying the contest was off. I underlined the word *off* three times. No explanation. How could I give one with so much to explain?

From the way Allison had complained about the contest yesterday, I expected her to be ecstatic. I certainly didn't expect her to corner me at recess and demand to know what was going on.

"Can't you read? I told you in my note! Forget it," I yelled. "I don't even care about the contest anymore."

"But why? Yesterday you were—"

"Yeah, and the day before, and the day before that too. But you know what? I don't care now. If you want to know the truth, I wish I never had. I wish you'd never talked me into going into Mr. Delvechio's in the first place. It's all your fault. I never would have known about the contest if it hadn't been for you."

"Whoa!" Allison's hands flew to her hips. "Excuse me. You were the one who wanted to win the trip to Disney World."

"He's not there," I screamed. "He's not even there."

"Who?"

"The man who's supposed to be my father. He's not anywhere in the whole state of Florida. I called the tour company where he said he'd be working, and they don't even know where he is." I couldn't help it. I was bawling my eyes out. "Nobody knows. Not even my mother or her lawyer. Obviously Dad doesn't want us to know. He doesn't care about us."

There was a long pause as I tried to catch my breath. In the distance I could hear the other kids whooping and hollering over an unimportant game of kickball. Meanwhile, Allison kept her face down and concentrated on giving pebbles little kicks.

"Gee, Steph," she said finally, "what a pain. And just when we were on the verge of winning the contest. Don't you even want to try?"

I couldn't believe her. She was supposed to be my best friend. "How can you be so dumb? What good is a trip to Disney World if my father isn't even there? You ought to be happy. Yesterday you were throwing fits over ice cream."

This time Allison didn't even bother rolling her eyes to let me know what she thought.

"Fine then. Here's me being happy." She started a jerky little dance, twirling around with her arms in the air and kicking up her heels. "So there. All right?" When she stopped, she put her hands back on her hips. She leaned forward until her nose was about an inch from mine. "I beg your pardon, Steph," she hissed. "But being around you the past couple of months has been like having my own personal storm cloud for a pet."

"You must have liked it," I shouted back. "I never heard you tell me not to come over."

"It's not like I had a choice," Allison jeered. "Your mother pays my mother. That's what she meant when she said she had to talk to your dad. He owes her a bundle."

"My mother pays you to be friends with me?"

"That's not what I said."

"It sure sounded like it."

"Shut up!" Allison shouted. "Maybe I ought to go over to Deidra's after school. She's invited me tons of times, and I always said I couldn't because of you."

How could Allison be so cruel? She was my friend, not Deidra's. "You can't go to Deidra's," I whispered.

"Can too."

"No, you can't. You have to have permission." It was the only thing I could think of.

"I'll call my mom."

"You can't. Your mom's taking Matthew to the doctor."

"No problem. I'll call my dad," Allison yelled over her shoulder, grinning as she stomped away.

After school I got off the bus by myself and trudged over to Allison's. She hadn't bothered to tell me that she was definitely going to Deidra's until right before the bell rang, when everyone was busy gathering up books and sweaters.

Deidra had pushed herself between us. "I'm so glad you can come, Allison. My mom said she'd take us to the mall. Afterward we can rent a movie or maybe two."

Deidra paused. "You *are* staying for dinner."

I didn't wait to hear Allison's answer but hurried out the front hall toward Mrs. Rogers' bus. I couldn't depend on my dad. Now I couldn't depend on my best friend.

Riding home on the bus without Allison, I felt as though I were coming down with the flu. My eyes burned. My shoulders ached. My chest hurt worst of all.

Mrs. Lampe was waiting at the front door, Matthew drooling on her hip. I could tell she felt very sorry for me.

"Come on. I got your favorite snack," she said as she followed me (slowly because I was really dragging my heels), her hand resting on my already heavy shoulder. "Get rid of your school bag and take Matthew for me."

She opened up the cabinet and pulled out a bag of Oreos and a plate. Then she poured milk into two tall glasses. Without being told, I eased Matthew's chubby little legs into his high chair and handed him a cookie. Ordinarily, I would have felt happy that Mrs. Lampe had thoughtfully bought my favorite cookies. But as I sat down at the kitchen table and started to chew, the chocolate tasted salty.

Mrs. Lampe kept looking kindly at me, as if she expected me to say something. When I didn't, she leaned forward and patted my hand. "Steph, I know it's been difficult for you and your mother since your father left."

I took another bite of salty Oreo and put it back on the plate, half-eaten. I sighed and then nodded.

"If you don't mind, I think I'll go upstairs and do my homework," I said.

"You're not going to be in the kitchen making ice cream?"

"I don't think so. Not today."

Mrs. Lampe's cool hand ran down the side of my face, checking for a fever. I'd seen the same concerned look in my mom's eyes countless times. It must be part of being a mom, I thought.

In Allison's room I wasn't sure I should lie across her pink bed. It looked so untouchable. Finally I folded the bedspread carefully all the way to the bottom and positioned myself sideways across the bed, with my feet hanging off the sides so they wouldn't touch the pink bedspread. I propped my history book open, but the print kept blurring. Finally I burrowed my head in Allison's pillow and cried.

When I finally fell asleep, I fell into a deep chocolate hole where Mr. Delvechio's entry blanks swirled around me like snow. I fell for miles, my arms grasping at nothing.

Feeling sorry for yourself can be awfully boring. When I woke up, I decided helping Mrs. Lampe with Matthew would be more fun. Besides, I'd noticed how tired she'd been looking lately, almost as tired as Mom.

I found her in the family room. She was folding laundry while Matthew bounced around in his walker. He was gurgling and making silly sounds to his fist. Once in a while he'd try to jam his fist in his mouth. When it didn't fit, he'd get frustrated. He'd screw up his face and get ready to cry. Then Mrs. Lampe would have to stop what she was doing and pick him up.

"Mrs. Lampe, sometimes my mom takes a bubble bath when she comes home from work. If you wanted, I could play with Matthew so you could take one now."

For a minute I thought Mrs. Lampe's mouth would fall off her face. Then her eyes turned shiny, and her cheeks puffed up just like a little girl's.

"Why, Stephanie, that's about the nicest present anyone's given me in a long while!" She jumped up. "Let me show you where I keep everything in his room. I'll be right here for you to ask if you need anything else."

I didn't say it, but I thought Mrs. Lampe was being silly. I'd been in her house practically every day since Matthew was born. I'd seen her warm his bottles at least a million times, but she still wanted to show me where she kept his diapers and what to do in case he got hungry. Finally she set me down in front of the TV and put Matthew in my lap.

Looking at Matthew's sweet little nose and his wide blue eyes made me wonder if my father had ever held me this close. I wondered if my hand had curled around his finger just as Matthew's was curling around mine. I was so deep in thought that when Mrs. Lampe came up behind the couch, she startled me.

"Mr. Lampe and I will be celebrating our anniversary this weekend. We wanted to go out for dinner. It's too bad you and Allison won't be available to baby-sit. You're so good with Matthew."

What was she talking about? "Why aren't we available?"

Mrs. Lampe hesitated. "Are you forgetting? There's a slumber party Saturday night."

"Whose slumber party?"

Mrs. Lampe came around the couch. She put her arm around me. "Oh, Stephanie, I'm sorry. I assumed you were invited. It's at Deidra's."

Unable to say anything, I shook my head no. How could I have been so stupid? I had been right there in the second-floor bathroom last Tuesday when Deidra handed Allison the pink party invitation. All this time, and Allison hadn't said a word.

Not wanting Mrs. Lampe to feel any worse than she already did, I took a deep breath. "How about if I baby-sit alone then?"

Mrs. Lampe sighed. "Are you sure your mother would allow it?"

"Sure," I said, though I really wasn't. "As long as it's only dinner and you and Mr. Lampe don't stay out really late."

I was surprised that my mother thought baby-sitting Matthew was a good idea. Of course, I didn't tell her that Allison wouldn't be baby-sitting with me. I didn't want her to worry about my being all alone in the Lampes' house at night with nothing but a sleeping baby and the TV for company. Mom had enough to think about with her exams coming up.

When I arrived at the Lampes' house, Allison let

me in. I took off my jacket and hung it on the hook in the foyer.

"I thought I'd be gone by now," Allison said, scooting her sleeping bag away from the door with her foot. "Deidra's parents are picking everyone up."

"Yeah, right," I said sarcastically. "Have a ball."

Just then I heard Mr. and Mrs. Lampe on the steps leading from the bedrooms. I had to catch my breath. I had never seen Mrs. Lampe so beautiful. She was wearing a blue silk dress and a string of pearls with matching earrings. As she came closer, I could smell her perfume. Then she smiled the biggest, most grateful smile I have ever seen. If I had any doubts about baby-sitting my former best friend's brother while my former best friend went to a slumber party without me, that smile made them disappear.

"This is so awkward," Mrs. Lampe said, her smile changing into a familiar look of concern as she glanced from Allison to me. For a moment I thought she felt worse about my being excluded from Deidra's slumber party than I did. "Allison, I thought Mr. Carroll was picking you up at seven. I don't like Stephanie having to see you off." She turned to Mr. Lampe and raised her eyebrows, questioning.

Mr. Lampe glanced nervously at his watch. "We have reservations. We can't wait any longer."

"Go on," Allison urged. "Deidra's parents will be here any minute. You'll probably pass them on your way out."

"Mrs. Lampe, I'm fine," I said in what I hoped was a convincing voice.

"Matthew is in his crib. You'll need to check him every once in a while. He only took a short nap this afternoon, so he should sleep soundly."

Mr. Lampe slipped a coat over her shoulders. "We won't be late. I left the phone number of the restaurant on the kitchen table."

"Don't worry. Matthew will be fine. You just have fun," I said.

Just as Mr. Lampe was about to open the door, he bent down and gave Allison a kiss on the forehead. As Allison's arms wrapped around his shoulders, my arms ached, wanting to do the same. I had to turn away.

Why, when I was doing so well without thinking of him, did my father have to pop up unbidden in my mind? Why couldn't he leave me alone?

My heart was still pounding as we stood at the front window and watched the car pull out of the driveway. The headlights had barely disappeared at the end of the street when I turned to Allison.

"You ought to stay here. How can you go without me?" I asked. It was the same question I wanted to ask my father.

"I can go very easily. You're not exactly fun anymore. And what's worse, you're a quitter."

My face burned with anger. "I'm not a quitter," I said between clenched teeth.

Allison tossed her head. "Yes, you are. You're quitting the contest. Well, I'm not a quitter. I want to go to Disney World too, and the only thing I want to find there is a big mouse. I've already decided. I'm entering one of our flavors."

"Over my dead body," I yelled, my face hotter than a raging forest fire.

It was a good thing for Allison that the phone rang, because I was about to pop her in the shoulder. This probably would not have been a good idea.

I stood there a minute, still seething, while I listened to Allison giggling on the phone. It wasn't as if I couldn't help myself. I knew what I was doing as I headed for the kitchen. When I opened the door to the freezer, I was even more sure.

Three at a time, I grabbed the Styrofoam cups filled with our flavors of ice cream and dumped them in the kitchen sink. Twenty-six Styrofoam cups with their black Magic Marker names stared up at me. Chocolate Madness, Peanut Brittle Chip, Lingonberry Delight. What did it matter?

I swung the faucet around and aimed it at the cups, then turned on the hot water full blast. The melted ice cream swirled down the drain, and with it all my hopes.

Allison screamed, "What are you doing? You are crazy! Do you know that?"

I turned to face her, too stunned to answer.

It was a good thing Allison was going to Deidra's.

The way I was feeling, I wasn't sure we could handle a whole evening together. In a trance I stumbled upstairs to check on Matthew.

Strangely enough, seeing Matthew blissfully asleep in his fuzzy zip-up pajamas calmed me. Maybe it was because, even if it was for only this one short evening, Matthew needed me to take care of him, something I knew I could do. Downstairs with Allison were reminders of too many things that had gone wrong: the contest, our friendship, my father.

Gently I moved Matthew's blanket away from his face, being careful to leave a small piece of satin binding crunched inside his tiny fist. Then I set his favorite stuffed animal in the corner of the crib where he would see it if he woke up. Leaving the night-light on in the hallway, I went back downstairs.

For the next half hour Allison and I could have been sitting on an iceberg instead of the couch in front of the Lampes' television. Every time I got halfway interested in a program, Allison thrust her arm straight out, pointed the remote at the screen, and *zap!* we were on a different channel.

By the time Deidra's parents arrived, I was glad to see Allison go. I was sure she'd tell everyone what a miserable time she had being stuck with me every day after school. She didn't even bother to say good night to me when she left. It was pretty obvious that we were through as friends.

Chapter 9

Sunday's Child

Sunday is my favorite day of the week. Mom is usually busy on Saturday mornings with errands. Then she stops by the library. Unless we go to a movie, she spends the night studying and taking notes on long sheets of yellow paper. After church on Sundays, though, we almost always do something together.

When I got up, Mom was still in bed. Her dark hair was a tangled mess, and newspapers were strewn across the covers. She had her cup of coffee on the nightstand and was leaning back against the headboard, her knees propped up like a grasshoppers.

"Good morning, sweetie." She tilted her head. "You don't look so good. What's wrong?" The newspapers she was reading collapsed like a tent. She held the covers open for me to climb in.

"Nothing."

"You're sure?"

I nodded, knowing she wouldn't believe me. Talking would only make it worse. Besides, I wasn't in the mood.

"Did you have a fight with Allison?"

I nodded glumly, amazed at how my mom always knows what's wrong. It must be ESP.

"You want to tell me about it?"

"Later," I said, giving the pillow a good smack.

Mom sighed. She waited a few minutes, then said, "I thought we'd go to the National Art Gallery. How does that sound?"

Now you may find this hard to believe, but the National Art Gallery is one of my favorite places. It's not just the paintings I like; it's the whole feeling of the place. It is so open and uncrowded. The rooms have polished wooden floors that give everything a honeylike glow. That, plus the quietness, makes me feel very peaceful.

That was probably why Mom had chosen the gallery, I thought as I snuggled beside her. After hearing that I'd had a fight with my best friend, she probably assumed I was in need of peaceful restoration.

"Don't you have to study?" I asked as Mom smoothed the blankets over my legs and put her arms around me. Tomorrow was her important exam.

"I'd rather be with you. I can study tonight after you go to bed."

"Ouch!" Now she was squeezing me too tightly.

"But, Stephanie, I love you!"

Sometimes it feels good when your mother says something mushy.

Impulsively I dug my fingers into her ribs and started to tickle. The bed squeaked as she folded her arms tight, protecting all the good places. Suddenly, just as I was about to stop, she reached out and yanked at the sheets. She grabbed my feet and ran her fingers across their bare bottoms. I fell backward on the mattress, kicking and gasping for breath.

"Tickle, tickle, tickle!" She giggled.

I screamed. Newspapers and blankets fell to the floor. My arm just missed her lamp.

Finally exhausted, Mom stopped. Her face was flushed and sweaty.

"How long do you think it'll take you to get ready? It's almost ten, lazybones, and we still have to go to church."

"I'll be ready before you are!" I made a dash for the shower, leaving Mom to clean up the mess we'd made in the bedroom.

After church we went straight to the Metro, which is a subway into the city. I always feel pretty smug riding it since I must have been on it at least a million times more than Allison. But never alone or with my dad. Always with my mother.

It wasn't long before we were wandering through the gallery, our sneakers squeaking against the wooden floors. Occasionally we'd stop in front of a painting, drinking in the beauty the artist had left behind on the canvas. Then we'd be on to another. I like afternoons like that.

Afterward, we went to the tearoom, where we sat at a round white table, just the two of us. It was very cozy, particularly when you don't get to spend as much time with your mom as you would like.

We ordered, and the waitress took our menus.

"So, tell me, Stephanie," my mom said, resting her elbows on the table, her fingers knitted together under her chin, "what is going on between you and Allison?"

I kept my head down and fiddled with the silverware. "Nothing. I just don't want to go there after school anymore, that's all," I said, my lip quivering.

Mom leaned across the table to pat my hand as a busboy filled our water glasses. "You and Allison are best friends. Something serious must have happened between you two."

I sniffed. Yeah, one day Allison and I are best friends, and the next day we aren't. I struggled to sort through my jumbled thoughts.

Just because I was angry at Dad for not writing, except for the one lousy postcard, and took it out on Allison. Just because Allison would rather go to Deidra's house instead of spend the afternoon with her own personal storm cloud. Just because I drove her crazy trying to win an important trip to Disney World so I could get my parents back together and make them a Tip Top Tour Team. Just because I quit trying to win the contest when I discovered my dad wasn't in Florida as he'd said he'd be. Just because Allison abandoned me to go to a slumber party instead of helping me baby-sit Matthew. Just because I poured our ice cream down the drain because I was jealous that she had a father and I didn't. What kinds of reasons were those to bust up a lifelong friendship? I tried to explain this to Mom.

Mom nodded as our waitress set our plates in front of us and said all the right things to keep me talking. Like "Mmm," "Tell me more," and "What else?" When I got to the part about the Tip Top Tour Team, she rubbed my arm and murmured, "Oh, sweetie, I'm so sorry," until there was hardly anything left for me to confess. All I had now were questions that Mom alone could answer. They were questions I'd been wanting to ask for a long time.

"I know how you and Dad met, but were you friends before you got married?" I said, looking shyly across the table. "When did you stop being friends?"

Of course, the real question I wanted to ask was "If you stopped being friends with each other, could you stop being friends with me?" but I hadn't worked up the nerve for that one. But that's the thing about talking to my mom. Sometimes even when you don't ask a particular question, it gets answered anyway.

Mom put her club sandwich back on her plate. "I guess you remember how I met your dad at a swimming pool, but I'm not sure if I ever told you I was going to an all-girl high school and considered myself pretty unattractive, even ugly. For some reason your dad thought differently. He was the first boy ever to ask me out."

"How old were you?"

Mom looked at me and then went on as though everything I'd asked were perfectly reasonable. As though I had a right to know.

"Sixteen. I was eighteen when we married."

I thought of Amy Sealander up the street, who was graduating from high school this year. She had a job and drove her own car, but she still didn't seem old enough to be married.

Mom wasn't finished. "Pops was in the army, so we traveled around a lot. We were always busy moving, and I was always switching schools, so I didn't have time to make many permanent friends. As a result, I grew up feeling left out, as though I didn't belong anywhere or to anyone. When your dad came along, he made me feel wanted. I could feel myself blossom with his attention. I felt secure and I trusted him. I thought at long last I had my first permanent friend."

As the busboy refilled our glasses, I remembered what Allison had said about Mike's being cute. "Is that what it's like . . . being in love?"

Mom nodded. "That's some of it. Your dad was very special. We went to movies and dances. Suddenly I was like all the other girls I went to high school with. They actually spoke to me in the hallways, all because some guy was taking me out."

"Gee."

"Yeah."

"What about Grandma and Pops?"

Mom squeezed a lemon wedge in her iced tea, added sugar, and slowly stirred. Even with the chatter and silverware clanking in the background, her spoon in her glass sounded loud. I waited to hear what she would say.

"They thought I was too young." She set the spoon on the table, looked at me, and smiled a little vacantly. "They wanted me to go to college. Instead your dad and I ran off and got married right after the senior prom. It was perfect. I had my fancy dress with shoes dyed to match, and your dad was so handsome in his rented tux. I used my corsage as my wedding bouquet. It was so romantic. Instead of going to the beach like everyone else, we went to Maryland and got married." Her voice drifted off.

"Were you ever sorry?"

"Well, sometimes, before I had you, I thought it might have been more fun to go to the beach. But I'm not sorry now. Not when I look at you." Mom's smile lit her face. "If I hadn't married your dad, I wouldn't have you, would I?"

She cleared her throat. "I just thought things would turn out differently, that's all. I think it's something that happens to a woman after she has a baby. Women want to settle down. For a while things were bright and cheerful. But the good days never seemed to last the way they should. It's the hardest thing, Stephanie, giving up on dreams." She straightened her shoulders. "But then, I think, I didn't give up. I only changed my priorities."

"Oh," I said, not exactly sure what she meant. I started to say as much, but then the waitress reappeared with the dessert menu.

"I'll have the cheesecake," Mom said. "What about you, Stephanie?"

I didn't need to peek at the menu to know what I wanted. "A double chocolate hot fudge sundae with extra sauce." I settled back in my chair.

Maybe it was because I had ordered ice cream, but before I knew it, I was telling Mom about Allison and me snooping in Mike's house, Mike's huge baby picture ("Naked, Mom, except for a teddy bear!"), and Mrs. Pierce's refrigerator loaded with DO NOT TOUCH notes, and Mike's 101 flavors.

"It's not fair," I said as I scooped the maraschino cherry and mounds of whipped cream from my dessert. I stared at the sea of chocolate fudge surrounding the mountain of rich chocolate ice cream. "Mike's got that super sorbet maker. Plus he's using his computer to make formulas. I don't care if Allison's mad at me. I was smart to dump all our ice cream down the drain."

Mom looked up from her cheesecake and frowned. "You make it sound as though you, Allison, and Mike are the only ones involved. I'm sure that isn't so."

"Yeah, yeah," I said, swallowing. "But if I had stopped to think of all the grown-ups who might have entered the contest, like chemistry professors, chiefs of police, or even the mayor, I never would have tried. Mike with his fancy machine was bad enough."

Mom chuckled. "Pooh on Mike and his machinery. You're the one with imagination. You can't beat that. To be honest, I'm disappointed to see you give up on something you put so much energy into."

I almost bolted out of my chair. "Mom, it's not going to be a habit. It's just this once. And if you expect me to reenter the contest, forget it! The deadline is tomorrow at 7:00 P.M. The only way I could possibly win now is if you bought me ten ice-cream machines and I had all of them going at the same time."

Mom immediately raised her eyebrows. "Wait a minute! Meaning, if I don't buy you those machines, it's my fault when you don't finish what you start?" She shook her head. "I don't think so, darling."

"Well, maybe not ten," I said weakly.

Mom's voice rose slightly. "Stephanie, you need to understand. I'm not being mean. But if I let you buy even one, chances are you'll think you need ten. And tomorrow you'll probably think you need twenty. After that, whenever you have a deadline, you'll panic, thinking you need something magical to bail you out." Mom blotted her mouth with her napkin. "Actually all you need to do before tomorrow evening is create one very special flavor."

I thought about what she said as I licked the last bit of double chocolate off my spoon. "But if I do reenter," I said slowly, "and I'm not saying I'm going to, I'd still need more of Mr. Delvechio's vanilla ice cream. Plus I'd need some ingredients, and I already tried everything in the supermarket. On our way home do you think we could stop at the international market in McLean?"

Mom pushed her chair back and signaled for our waitress. "Come on, sweetie. If we hurry, you can create a flavor or two before bedtime."

As the subway rumbled under the streets of Washington, D.C., taking us back to the station close to home, I made up my mind. Even if the prize was no longer important, the contest was. I'd started it, and I was going to finish it. It was something I had to prove to myself and to Mom. I was not a quitter.

"Boy, this looks complicated," Mom said, coming up behind me as I smushed Mr. Delvechio's vanilla with my assorted ingredients.

I shrugged. "Yeah. You would think this was the hard part."

"It isn't?" Mom sounded surprised.

"No! According to Mrs. Pierce, choosing which of your flavors to enter is the hardest. You can enter only one. That's why, in my opinion, what Mike is doing is really sneaky. He invited everyone to his house tomorrow to judge his flavors. The rumor is everyone who goes has to sign a pledge promising not to steal his winning flavor."

"Sounds serious."

"It is."

"Mike's going to make up his mind on the basis of what everyone else decides?"

"Yep. They're going to vote."

"Then it doesn't sound like Mike's decision anymore. I'm not sure I'd like it that way."

"No. But it's easier than deciding yourself. With so many people you can't make a mistake."

"Stephanie," Mom said, "everyone makes mistakes. Just recently I made a pretty big one not recognizing that you were old enough to stay home by yourself."

I could hardly believe it.

"You won't worry?"

"No more than I do anyway. You'll call me when you get home, right?"

"Yeah."

"And you would call Mrs. Lampe if you had an emergency, right?"

"You bet." I brightened. Things were really looking up.

Chapter 10

April Fool

"Okay, everyone! You can't get into Mike's party unless you sign one of these pledges." Allison was outside our classroom, standing in the middle of a group of girls and waving a bright yellow paper in the air.

It was before the morning bell. I wouldn't exactly say I was hiding, but from where I was crouched down in the coat cupboard I doubted she—or any of the other girls, Deidra included—could see me.

"You can't use a pencil. And no markers. It has to be pen," Allison went on. "And sign your whole name. Neatly. Don't forget to date it. And don't put Monday," she added. "It has to be April first."

One of the girls giggled. "Can't we just put April Fool's Day on it?"

"Who made up these things?" someone asked. "Where'd they come from? I didn't know it was *your* party. I thought it was Mike's."

Allison blushed. "It's not. I mean, it is," she stammered. "Mike's father had the pledges printed up at his office. It was his mother's idea."

A murmur went through the crowd.

"And in case you're wondering . . ." Deidra sashayed through the crowd to stand next to Allison. "Mike spent hours on the phone with Ali explaining everything."

Ali! I almost barfed in someone's boot. Weren't they just too chummy!

"I was there when he brought the pledges over to her house last night," Deidra went on. "And I personally witnessed it when he put Allison in charge of the girls." She paused while everyone took this in. "It has to be April first. April Fool's Day isn't legal."

Allison looked up, and for a long horrible moment I thought she'd spotted me kneeling among the jackets and book bags. She frowned for a second and squinted, but I ducked quickly to the right and hid behind an ugly itchy wool sweater that had been in the closet ever since we'd come back after Christmas vacation. I pulled the sweater closer to my face and tried not to sneeze as a couple of the girls carried their pledges over to a table for signing.

I watched as they returned the completed forms to Allison, who folded them neatly before slipping them into a big white envelope with "PP" drawn on it in fancy green letters. Everybody in our class knew that the "PP" stood for Pierce's Perfections.

"This party is going to be so cool," one of Deidra's friends said as several of them passed the coat closet on their way to the classroom.

"Can you imagine what it's going to be like?" asked another. "My mom says we should be sure to swish our mouths with water between flavors so we don't get them confused."

"I've been practicing."

"Is it true that Mrs. Pierce is going to wheel everything out on a gourmet cart?" someone called back to Allison.

What a stupid question, I thought. Winning Mr. Delvechio's contest didn't have anything to do with Mrs. Pierce's cart.

"Probably she wants to make up for all those DO NOT TOUCH! signs," someone else quipped.

Uh-oh, I thought. Allison had been spilling the beans about the Pierces' refrigerator. Not a very nice thing to do.

"Mike didn't say anything about his mother's cart," Allison answered without so much as batting an eye. "But the flavor sampling is going to be very professional. We'll have scorecards and everything."

"Yes," Deidra interjected. "Who knows? They might even name the flavor after one of us."

"Well, I don't know about that," Allison said quickly. "But we'll probably get some kind of credit."

"Do you think they'll make a commercial with us in it?" one of the girls asked.

Just then I felt the most horrible tickle. I pinched my nose and blocked a giveaway sneeze.

"Is anybody bringing a camcorder?" Deidra asked. "Someone better call her mom and ask."

"How many flavors did Mike say? How many are we responsible for? Honestly, Mike is just a winner all the way around."

Everyone in the group nodded while I snorted at the last comment. The heck with them and their stupid party, I thought as I backed out of the closet. I was already excited about today, but for an entirely different reason.

This afternoon after school I was finally going home—straight home, not to Allison's. Forget the fact that Mom was taking the day off from work to study for a major test. I was still letting myself in with my own key. Mom had promised to study in her room so I could at least pretend to be on my own. For someone who didn't like to make changes in huge steps, Mom was being awfully brave.

I was thinking about all this while trying to keep my head down as I slid my books into my desk. But from the corner of my eye I could see the bright yellow forms floating up and down the aisles. I groaned. It was going to be a long day.

"Hey, Pierce," Harvey hollered from across the room, "my mother says we have to unload the ice cream in our mouths without tasting the plastic on the spoon. Is that true?"

"No problem for you, water-bucket mouth," Nick bellowed. It was a good thing Mrs. Simpson wasn't in the room yet.

"Yeah. And don't chew any gum after school," Tyrone added.

By now almost all the girls had filtered into the classroom. Knowing the bell would ring soon, I started back for the coat cupboard to hang up my backpack, passing Tonya and some other girls on the way.

"The first thing I'm going to do is pretend to go to the bathroom so I can eyeball Mike's baby picture in the hall," Tonya was saying.

Whoa! I wondered if Mike would be so snowed by Allison if he knew she had blabbed about his bare bottom.

I found an empty hook for my backpack. I had just started toward the classroom when Allison's giggle stopped me short. I turned around.

Allison and Deidra were bent over the table, their heads together as they alphabetized the signed pledges and checked them off against a class roster. Allison stacked the remaining forms on the table very efficiently.

"I'm still pooped from your slumber party." Allison leaned back and yawned. "I hope I don't fall asleep in class. I guess I'll have to wait until this afternoon for Mike's ice cream to perk me up."

Deidra reached inside her purse. "Oh, I almost forgot. You left your tape beside my stereo."

"Thanks," Allison said, taking it. "Remember what we decided. The next party is at my house."

"Soon," Deidra said. "Promise?"

"Sure. Anyway I'm glad you're riding the bus home with me so we can go to Mike's together. Normally I'd be going with Stephanie, but you know . . ."

Hearing my name, I cocked my head farther in their direction. Even though it had only been one-and-a-half days since our big fight, I expected Allison to say how much she missed hanging around with me. Surely she was going to apologize for ignoring me and being such an all-around stubborn brat.

"Speaking of Stephanie," Deidra said, "did you see her earlier? I swear she is so weird. She was hiding in the coat closet. Talk about juvenile. She was peeking behind that ugly sweater my grandmother sent me for Christmas."

I could feel myself blush. I wasn't weird or juvenile. Surely Allison would defend me. We'd been best friends since kindergarten. But she said nothing.

Deidra shrugged her shoulders. "So, what have you and Mike decided to do about Stephanie?"

I held my breath as Allison put the last of the signed pledges in the green and white envelope.

"As far as I'm concerned, she's not invited," Allison remarked with a snippy toss of her head. "I'm not even talking to her until she apologizes."

I bit my lip to keep from screaming. Apologize, my foot. I'd show them.

"What's this, Ali?" I said, ambling up to the table. This was a challenge I couldn't resist.

If she was startled to see me, she didn't let on. Instead she looked me right in the eye and raised her left eyebrow. "It's Allison to you," she said flatly.

I shrugged. "Whatever."

Then, just as I was reaching for one of those stupid flaming yellow pledges, Allison brought her hand down on what was left of the stack. If I'd truly wanted one—of course, I didn't—I would have had to fight her for it. It was hardly worth the effort.

"You don't get one," Allison snarled as she crammed the blank pledges in the envelope and sealed it tight.

Under the circumstances what else could I do? I gave them my loudest raspberry, turned my back, and, with my head held high, marched into the classroom.

During our afternoon break I noticed Mike watching me. I was by myself, the class outcast, and he cut himself from a group of boys to join me.

"I have something for you. I thought maybe we could be friends now that you quit the contest." He held out one of those sickening yellow forms.

I kept my hands behind my back. No way was I going to take one of those pledges. But at least now I could say I'd been invited.

"Mike Pierce, I wouldn't sign that slip of paper if my life depended on it," I said haughtily. "And for your information I am not a quitter. I'm still in the contest."

"Yeah, right, Kulik. With what? We all know you dumped your flavors down Allison's drain."

I sucked in my breath. How embarrassing. My former best friend had betrayed me. Everyone in the classroom was probably laughing about my temper tantrum.

"Listen," I said, "none of those flavors was good enough. I decided that for myself. I didn't need the whole school to help me make up my mind. For all you know, there's an excellent chance that the winning flavor is sitting in my freezer right now."

Mike stepped back to laugh. He glanced at the crowd that had assembled around us.

"You don't scare me. I have one hundred and seven flavors in *my* freezer. All of them are winners. What do you say, guys?"

A ripple of support ran through the crowd.

I looked at blabbermouth Allison, who was standing next to Deidra.

"Big deal," I said. "You have one hundred and seven losers. I have the winning flavor."

Hands on hips, Mike stepped closer. "That's for Mr. Delvechio to decide."

"Yeah, and you can bet he won't be picking anything with your name on it. Get this, Michael Pierce," I said, mimicking his know-it-all tone as best I could. "This time you're going to lose."

"Says who?" Mike leaned closer, practically shoving his nose in my face.

"Says me!"

There is nothing that draws a teacher faster than a crowd on the playground. Mrs. Simpson appeared from out of nowhere. The next thing I knew, we were back in the classroom doing stinky math problems.

I bent my head low over my paper and, using pink and brown markers, drew a line of ice-cream cones, two scoops each. Despite what I'd said on the playground, I knew I didn't have the winning flavor. I couldn't go to Mike's party even if I had wanted to. I had to get home, do some big-time inventing, write the whole recipe down, and rush it over to Mr. Delvechio's by 7:00.

Picking up my pencil, I began to write flavor names, hoping to get inspired. When I reached the bottom of the page, I began another. Once, looking up, I found Mrs. Simpson smiling at me.

"Almost done, Stephanie?" she asked.

I was too embarrassed to answer.

Just then the bell rang. Dismissal.

The only thing that made the ride home anywhere near bearable was knowing that I would never have to go to Allison's house again. Otherwise I still felt pretty miserable, staring out the window with no one to talk to while Allison yakked away in the back of the bus with Deidra. Allison would probably never be my friend again now that she was officially part of Deidra's in-group.

Blinking back tears, I tried to decide which of my new concoctions to try next for the contest. So far I didn't have the foggiest idea, and it was already 3:15.

We pulled over at the bus stop before mine. The doors screeched open, then closed again. My eyes followed the parade of little kids, all waving school papers and swinging lunchboxes as they safely crossed the street. From there I stared up East Street a bit, daydreaming. That's when I noticed a white limousine parked in front of our house.

Dad!

Chapter 11

How's My Girl?

I could hardly wait for the bus to stop. In fact, I didn't. Instead I bulldozed my way up the aisle to crowd the door. When it sprang open, I leaped forward, the first one off.

My feet never touched the sidewalk. I flew the whole way. I took the porch steps and pulled at the door without bothering with my key. Dad wouldn't lock me out.

Breathless, I slammed the door behind me.

Dad was sitting in the living room in the same wingback chair where he used to throw his coat. My mom sat stiffly on the couch across from him. When I saw him there, my heart leaped into my throat. Swallowing was impossible.

"Steph!" Dad stood, his arms outstretched.

"Daddy!" My voice was a little girl's.

He held me, his hand stroking the back of my head as I breathed in the sweet smell of his aftershave and tried not to sob like a baby. "I knew you would come home."

I stepped back and shivered with joy. He was so handsome in his designer tennis togs, the afternoon sun reflecting on his gold necklace while his deep tan set off his twinkling blue eyes.

For the moment I ignored the fact that I'd never seen him in tennis shorts before. And when he'd left, he hadn't had that gold necklace, or the tan.

Who cared? It was great to have him home again! Mom looked excited, too, sitting forward on the couch in her short skirt and blouse, her black hair blown around her face like a cloud and her cheeks romantically red.

I glanced from Dad to Mom and blushed.

"Oh, excuse me," I giggled. "I hope I'm interrupting something."

For a second no one said a word.

"So, how's my girl?" Dad said, finally breaking the awkward silence. He handed me his usual imported chocolate bars.

How's my girl? It was a phrase I'd heard as long as I could remember. When I heard it now, even as angry as I had been at Dad for not answering my letters, shivers ran up and down my back.

Mom stood up and motioned to Dad. "Reid, I think you have some explaining to do to Stephanie," she said in a sharp voice that startled me. When she turned to me and picked up her books, her voice was softer. "Sweetie, I'll be in the kitchen studying. If you need anything . . . "

I glanced at them, unsure. Why should I need Mom? Dad was home, wasn't he? Things were back to normal. Or were they?

Then I noticed that Mom had turned the sound down on the TV, leaving the images flickering across the screen. Maybe she'd been studying for her exam with the TV on since she can't study in complete silence. I wondered if my father had called before coming. Then I remembered how he'd never managed to find a phone before and figured he hadn't. He had probably surprised her as much as me.

No wonder she didn't know how to act. I knew how she felt. All along I had been anxious to see him, but now that he was here, I didn't know what to say or do. The only thing I knew for certain was that he was home and I would do anything to keep him here.

But Dad wasn't acting the way I'd expected. It was as though he couldn't decide what he should do or say either. The funny thing was even though his chair had been moved countless times while he was away, today it just happened to be in the very spot it had been in when he left. Sitting there, he could pretend he'd never left. He could ask casually about my math grade. Had we had a test today? He'd never have to say a word about Florida or Hilton Head or wherever he'd been.

"You look different," I said, puzzled, not meaning the tan but something else entirely. Then I saw he'd changed his hair. No longer did it flop in his face. It was short now, pushed up off his forehead like someone in a poster. Definitely not someone's father. Not mine anyway.

"I do?" He laughed, obviously considering this a compliment. "So, how's my girl anyway?"

He opened his arms again, expecting a bigger hug. I startled myself by stepping back.

I can't say how much it hurt to swallow. I struggled to keep my voice from squeaking. "Didn't you miss me?" I asked.

"Miss you? Of course, I missed you. I missed you so much, Steph. I tried to call you, but it caused too much pain. I couldn't stand the thought of hearing your voice and not seeing your face. Or being with you. Mom's the lucky one, you know. She's got you."

"What about me, Dad? Don't you think I hurt?"

"I know, Steph. Forgive me. I should have called. But I just couldn't. Here."

He reached behind the chair and held out a present wrapped in raspberry pink tissue paper and set in a shiny silver bag tied with a matching raspberry ribbon. "Here. A friend of mine designs these things."

"Oh, Dad," I sighed.

"I know, I didn't have to, princess, but you deserve it for putting up with your old man."

"You're not so bad. Anyway we got your postcard." It was a stupid thing to say, acting as if his sending one postcard could make up for months of not letting

Mom and me know where he was. Or sending us some money.

Still, I didn't want to say anything that would make him angry and give him an excuse to leave us again.

"Yeah, well. I looked around for a better postcard. There sure wasn't much to choose from. It was either golfers or tennis bums. Sunsets are real big."

"What about the tourist places where you gave all the tours?"

Embarrassed, he cleared his throat.

"You said you were going to Florida when you left," I added.

"Oh, yeah. Well . . ." He ran his hand through his hair, as though he were still training it to stand up rather than flop waterfall style as it was inclined to do.

"I did go to Florida. For a while at least." He glanced helplessly toward the kitchen. Did he want Mom to bail him out? Or did he not want her to hear?

"The truth of it is, after two weeks I got tired of Florida," he said finally. "Then, as luck would have it, I met someone who needed a ride. The first time I darn near forgot how cold it is here in the winter. I came all the way with nothing but a pair of jeans and a couple of shirts. Not even a jacket. It was pretty cold here in January, you know."

"You were here in January?" I could barely get the words out, but Dad didn't notice.

"Yeah, twice. Just for a couple days, though. You'd be surprised how many people are afraid to fly. They can't be bothered with a bus, so they pay you to drive them in their own car. Let me tell you, though, I was glad to get back and see the sunshine. You can't beat those beaches either." He paused, misinterpreting the dazed look on my face.

"Steph, snap out of it! Let's get moving. I planned a wonderful afternoon with my best girl. I thought we'd go to Georgetown Tennis and Racket and play a few sets. Afterward we'll get a bite to eat in the grill. You'll like it there. Everyone does," he said, shoving the present at me. "It's fancy. Skylights. Brass railings. The whole nine yards."

"But, Dad, didn't you come home to help me with the contest? Maybe you didn't realize that the deadline is today. Seven o'clock."

Dad frowned. "What contest?"

I gulped. "Dad, I can't believe you said that. You know, the ice-cream contest with Mr. Delvechio."

"Delvechio, the ice-cream man, is running a contest?" Dad started to laugh. "What kind of contest could he have?"

"Come on, Dad! Stop teasing," I pleaded. "The new flavor contest. It's all Allison and I have been doing, inventing ice cream."

"Hey, you and Allison are ice-cream inventors?"

"Well, not quite. That's why you've got to help. I thought that's why you came home. I wrote you all about the contest. In practically every let—" I stopped. Why hadn't it occurred to me? Dad had never even read my letters.

I tried hard to think why. Could it be that the lady at Sunshine Tours was holding them with all of his other mail? Was it possible there was a dead mailman in Florida like the one in McLean? Of course, I knew better than to ask Dad about either of these things.

I didn't want to make him angry. Now that he was in the house, I wanted to keep him here. "Why don't we work on the contest today?" I said brightly. "Who knows? Maybe we'll even get lucky and win. We can play tennis tomorrow. We'll have more time."

Dad fidgeted with his gold chain. "Well, it's a little more complicated than that. I have a friend who's going to meet us for dinner."

I shrugged. "No problem. Have him come here. Do you have his number? You could call him."

Dad rubbed his chest nervously. "I would, but I don't think your mother would appreciate that."

"You mean because she's studying?" Wasn't it nice of Dad to be thinking of Mom? "It's okay," I reassured him. "She can go in the bedroom and study. She does it all the time. Besides, I'm a pretty good cook now. I'll make chili. You have your friend's number, don't you? Go ahead. Call him."

"Steph," Dad said slowly, "you don't understand. My friend is a lady."

The Awful Truth

In one split second my whole world crashed in front of my eyes. Dad was right about one thing: I didn't understand.

"How come you need a lady friend?" I demanded. "Mom's in perfectly good health!"

"You don't understand," he said again. "It's what people do when they get a divorce. They go on dates. They make new friends."

"You're never going to change," I shouted, ignoring the *d* word. Why would Dad need new friends when he had Mom and me? "You never know who and what are important."

"Come on, princess," Dad pleaded as he reached into the bag with the raspberry ribbon. "Open your present. My friend designed it especially for you. We're hoping it's the right size so you can wear it this afternoon when we play. Look, it's your favorite color. Yellow."

How much could he hurt me? I was discovering it was a lot. Tons.

"Yeah, Dad," I said dryly. "Yellow is my favorite color all right, but I don't play tennis. You should know that." I would never admit the real truth: that I'd have to be dead before I'd wear something his new lady friend had even laid a finger on.

Dad blushed through his tan and smiled sheepishly. "So, what's wrong with trying new things? Hey, I even brought you a racket. Forget about the contest. Let's hop in the old limo. I already picked up a couple of court passes. It'll be just you and me, like old times. What do you say?"

Angrily I stuffed the outfit back into the bag and looked him right in the eye. "I can't forget the contest. I'm committed. You see, Dad, when you left, I discovered something important about myself. I am not a quitter."

Dad cleared his throat. "The problem is, princess, I'm in town only for today. Sure you won't change your mind?" he asked, taking out his keys.

My heart was banging in my chest so loudly I thought he must have heard as I handed him back the present.

"I'm positive."

Dad stepped back toward the door. I'd never seen him look the way he did at that moment. He was stunned. "I guess I'll have to try to phone you later."

In a million years how could I believe him?

The smell of his aftershave lingered in the air as I

125

bit my lip to keep from crying and watched him go.

Feeling like a burst balloon, I plopped my books on the kitchen table where Mom was studying.

"Mom, he never even read my letters."

Her eyes were bloodshot. "I know. I heard. I'm sorry."

I rested my head on Mom's shoulder and let her gently rub my back.

"What you did was hard, sweetie. And very grown-up. I'm proud of you," she said softly.

"I don't even believe him, Mom," I said, straightening. "He tried to give me a present from a total stranger. It was like he was buying me off or something."

Mom nodded. She understood. "Darling, I'd give anything to have been able to protect you from what you're feeling now. I'd give anything not to have you hurt."

Almost afraid to look at her, I fiddled with my backpack. "Dad's never going to change, is he?"

"Probably not."

"You guys aren't getting back together either, are you?"

Mom shifted in her seat. "No, darling."

I thought about it for a long moment before asking, "Do you think I'll ever see him again?"

I kept my head down so she couldn't see my chin quivering, but it was no use. Mom knew.

"Leave your backpack alone, and look at me, Stephanie," she said.

Our eyes connected. From the tone of her voice I

knew her answer was going to be hard to take. But at least I knew she would treat me with respect by telling me the truth.

"I definitely think you'll see him again, although I couldn't say when exactly. Before you came home from school, your father and I had a short talk. He promised to send you a note every month along with his child support payment."

"But will he?"

Mom shrugged. "I can't say for sure, but I think there's a good chance that he will." Then, turning a page, she went back to her book.

Like a robot, I opened the cabinet doors and began pulling out the ingredients we had purchased the day before. With a sigh I set Dad's candy bars on the counter beside Mr. Delvechio's pink entry blank. I still wasn't sure what I would make.

I kept staring at the candy bars. Ever since I could remember, Dad had brought those candy bars home for me. They weren't the kind you got on Halloween or found in a regular supermarket.

There was no getting past it. My dad had turned out to be a big disappointment.

The strange thing was, I knew I still loved him. I didn't like how he treated Mom and me. I didn't like how he always let us down or how he was totally irresponsible and selfish. But the fact was, I had only one father. He was mine no matter what. And I still loved him.

I wiped a tear from my eye with the back of my hand.

"Mom," I said, turning, "maybe it sounds silly, but did you ever think how Dad is a lot like these candy bars?"

If Mom thought that what I was saying sounded weird, she never let on. Or maybe after the past couple of days she was getting used to strange things flying out of my mouth and figured the best way to deal with me was to let me ramble on.

"No, sweetie. I can't honestly say I ever thought of your father that way."

Frowning, I slowly peeled the wrapper from one of the candy bars. When Mom refused the square of chocolate I offered, I handed her the wrapper instead. For some reason, it was important that she understand.

"See, Dad was special," I explained as Mom looked at me curiously. "Just like these candy bars that you can't find anyplace around here. Otherwise why would you have put up with him?"

Mom jerked back in her chair, startled.

"I'm not saying you were wrong, Mom," I said quickly, not wanting to hurt her feelings any more than they'd already been hurt today. "But you *did* put up with him. You got awfully angry at him some-times. I remember all the fights. But you still put up with him."

"Yes, I did because separation and divorce aren't

something you enter into easily. It took a great deal of thought and torment on my part before I reached a decision."

"Cool it, Mom. I'm not blaming you or anything. Don't you see? The fact that it was such a hard decision proves how Dad is special, just like this candy bar."

Mom nodded as if maybe she hoped I was finished and she could safely go back to her homework. Then the rich and tantalizing chocolate aroma gave me another brainstorm.

"He's exotic, too!" I said. "Nobody ever knows what Dad is going to do next. Sometimes he was like a knight in shining armor or the prince in a fairy tale. Look at the way he showed up with that limousine and took me out on a date. He always made you feel when you were with him that you and he were part of another world. Maybe it was a make-believe world," I said slowly, "but it was exotic."

Mom put her pencil down again. She wouldn't admit it, but I could tell she agreed. "I think you might just be looking for an excuse to eat those candy bars, Stephanie."

"No, Mom," I insisted. I was on a roll. "Here's another one. Dad is smooth. I mean, *really* smooth." I waved the candy bar in front of her face. "Just like this milk chocolate. Dad is one smoo-oooth cookie."

Mom laughed. Unable to study, she was reading the brown and gold wrapper. "Yes," she finally said.

"Like milk chocolate. Definitely smooth."

Suddenly we were playing a game that Allison and I used to play. One person says a word, and the other person says the first thing that pops into her head. Only this time instead of Allison and me being goofy about school, it was Mom and me both howling about Dad.

"Hazelnut," Mom said.

"Can't eat just one," I said. "I could never get enough of Dad."

"Semisweet."

I sighed as I edged toward serious truth. "Roller coaster. One minute with Dad I was on top of the world. The next minute he let me down, leaving me with bittersweet memories." I chuckled to myself. "No wonder I like chocolate so much."

The wrapper fluttered to the floor as Mom stood up to hug me.

"You're absolutely right, sweetie. It's been quite a ride." She paused. "Are you okay now? If you are, I really do need to study. And what about your winning flavor?"

What Mom said was true. We couldn't be thinking about Dad now. We both had deadlines to meet. Mom had an exam to pass, and I had the contest. Neither of us was competing for a prize. We were competing for ourselves.

But what flavor could I invent?

Suddenly the answer screamed inside my head.

Chocolate! Chocolate! CHOCOLATE!

Why hadn't I thought of it before?

It would be exciting to use these special, exotic, and oh-so-smooth chocolate bars in my ice-cream flavor. The only problem was, which flavor should I use? They all were delicious.

If only there were more time, I thought desperately. Then I could invent four different chocolate ice-cream flavors and submit my first choice.

I checked my watch. I had only enough time to make one flavor.

I stared hard at the chocolate bars, knowing I had to plan my recipe very carefully. Finally, after setting the hazelnut and the semisweet bars in the freezer, I pulled out two pots. I filled the larger one with water and put it on the stove to boil. Then I put the milk chocolate bar in the smaller pot and set it over the boiling water. It was something I'd seen Mrs. Lampe do. When the milk chocolate melted, I mixed it with Delvechio's vanilla.

Mmm. A creamy milk chocolate base.

But I wasn't anywhere near finished.

I opened the freezer and tested the chocolate bars. They weren't frozen solid, but they were hard enough. I got out the vegetable peeler, a cheese shredder, measuring cups, and the cutting board.

I unwrapped the candy bars and got to work peeling and scraping. I brushed the grated chocolate and chocolate curlicues into measuring cups, took notes, and then stirred them into the chocolate ice cream.

Finally I melted the bittersweet chocolate bar and swirled thick gobs into the chocolate ice cream.

Feeling more confident than I'd ever felt before, I packed most of my new flavor into the Styrofoam cup Mr. Delvechio had provided. I wrote my name and phone number on the lid and stuck it in the freezer. The rest of my creation went into one of our cereal bowls. I carefully laid plastic wrap on top and put it in the freezer, too.

While waiting for the ice cream to freeze, I finished filling out the pink entry blank. I listed the ingredients and neatly printed the entire recipe. There was only one thing left to do. I had to name my new flavor.

Ten minutes later I sampled it. Just to be sure I wasn't dreaming, I closed my eyes and took another spoonful. I let the special, exotic, smooth chocolate concoction slowly spread its sweetness down my throat.

"Mom, come try this!" I shouted. "Now!"

A grin spread across my face as Mom tasted my new flavor.

"This is it, kiddo! Congratulations! It's fantastic! What are you going to call it?"

I struck a pose to make my grand announcement.

"I'm going to call it . . . Chocolate Daze."

 **Chapter 13**

Chocolate Daze Forever

"Mom, c'mon," I hollered as I bounded up the stairs. "We're going to be late."

It had been three weeks since my dad dropped the bombshell in our living room. Right after that I'd stopped writing to him. What I mean is, I stopped writing to him every day. It seemed a little lopsided, my writing to him all the time and his answering only with a short note when he sent Mom a check.

When the first check arrived yesterday, Mom tried to hide her surprise. I tried to hide my surprise too, when I found his note tucked inside.

> Hey, Steph—
> How's my girl? Sorry we didn't have a chance to play tennis. Maybe next time?
> My trip back to Hilton Head was not as sunny as the trip to D.C. Maybe that was because I didn't have your smiling face to

think about as I was driving. I think about you a lot, though, princess, and I just thank my lucky stars I have a girl like you to keep me straight. You are my greatest treasure.

Hope you're thinking about me.

Love,
Dad

Reading the note, I'd felt kind of sorry for him, but I still didn't feel the urge to tell him what I was doing absolutely every minute of every day. I knew that if he could walk away from Mom and me, he'd probably walk away from his new lady friend, too. He'd probably wind up being one of those people without a friend to their name. Mom says it has to do with growing up and making commitments. It's harder for some people than others. That's one reason why it was so important to keep my commitment to Mr. Delvechio's contest.

Today the whole town would finally know the outcome.

I was glad Mr. Delvechio had picked a Saturday to announce the winner of his contest so that everyone, even the grown-ups who had entered, could come. I particularly wanted to see the expression on Mom's face when I handed her the all-expense-paid tickets to Disney World. Just because my father wasn't there didn't mean we couldn't go and have a good time. The other face I wanted to see was Mike's.

What Mr. Delvechio had planned at the shopping center had turned into an extravaganza. Everything was to start at precisely 2:00 P.M., and I didn't want to miss a minute.

I'd done all my chores plus some of Mom's while she went to the grocer's. It wasn't hard. Now that I came straight home after school instead of going to Allison's, things didn't pile up anymore.

And now that Mom was no longer switching the furniture around, I felt a lot more settled. I didn't realize how insecure I had felt never knowing what our house would look like when I got up each morning.

We hadn't started redecorating my bedroom yet, but we had started on the living room. Last Saturday I helped Mom carry Dad's old chair out to the curb in time for our town's spring cleanup. We didn't have another chair to take its place, but we did have a stack of furniture catalogs. Mom said we didn't have to decide overnight. We could take our time and be choosy.

I called Mom again.

"I'm coming." Mom grabbed her purse off the chair and slung it over her shoulder. She had her keys out as she glanced in my direction. "Stephanie, in all the excitement you forgot to brush your hair."

Laughing at my own forgetfulness, I hurried toward the bathroom.

"Here, let me do it."

Mom stood behind me at the mirror. She took a brush out of the vanity drawer and began to smooth the tangles with sure strokes. Next, she held my hair in the back and turned it under.

"Close your eyes, sweetie," she said, tilting my head downward. She gave my hair a swoosh of spray, tickling my neck and giving me goose bumps.

What she said gave me goose bumps, too.

"I just want you to know that regardless of the outcome this afternoon, I'm very proud of you. When you do your best, you're always a winner. Besides that, you were persistent. You knew what you wanted and kept after it even when you thought about quitting."

I could feel Mom smoothing my bangs and fluffing out the sides.

"The important thing is that you didn't give up."

I wondered if she was thinking of my father and how he never stuck with anything. I wondered if she was glad I wasn't turning out like that. I knew I was.

Two more swooshes of the cold spray, and she was finished. When I opened my eyes, I was pleased by what I saw.

"Mom, it's beautiful."

"No," she answered, kissing me lightly on the cheek. "*You're* beautiful."

"Mom!" I could feel myself blush. "We're going to be late."

The parking lot was jammed. So was Mr. Delvechio's. As Mom and I worked our way through the crowd, I counted six teenagers making cones for his customers. A stage with pink and brown streamers had been set up on the sidewalk. Freckles the Clown was handing out free balloons.

I spotted Mike in the first row nearest the stage. I also saw Mr. Delvechio making his way through the crowd, stopping to talk to mothers with small children. When someone whispered in his ear, Mr. Delvechio responded by tapping the brown-and-pink envelope sticking out of his coat pocket. I shivered with excitement, knowing that was where the winner's name was. At the same time, Mike laughed. Clearly he was ready to accept his trip to Disney World.

"There's some open space beside the hot dog stand," Mom shouted above the music coming over the loudspeaker. "We can get ice cream later."

Together we inched our way toward the hot dog stand, passing Allison on the way. She was with Deidra and Tonya and a group of girls wearing makeup and flashy jewelry. If Mom saw Allison and thought she didn't belong with that crowd, she didn't say a word. I noticed how Allison was standing on the edge of the group. She wasn't the center of attention. Deidra was. Allison looked pathetic and miserable. I could relate to that. In three weeks Allison and I had hardly spoken to each other.

"It looks as if we might have time for a hot dog."

Mom turned from me to Allison. "Hi, Allison. Are you hungry?" she asked casually. "Would you like to join us?"

While Mom stood in line at the cash register, Allison and I took our hot dogs and drinks to a nearby table. I was squirting mine with mustard when Allison said shyly, "I hope you win today."

Not knowing what to say, I kept squirting. Suddenly I realized what I was doing.

"Yuck!" we both shrieked at once.

"You're not going to eat that mustard dog!" Allison giggled. "You hate mustard."

"I know." It was nice to be with someone who knew what I liked and didn't like. "I don't know what I'm doing," I confessed. "I'm so nervous."

"I know what you mean," Allison said. "My mom will kill me if she catches me hanging out with Deidra and her friends. I've been trying to get away from them, but I didn't know where to go."

"But Deidra's been at your house. I thought you two were really tight."

Allison laughed. "Not anymore. Not since my mom and I really got to know Deidra."

I rolled my eyes. "That'll do it. Anyway you can stay with us if you want," I said. "You can be in charge of bringing my mom back to consciousness when I go up on the stage. Okay?"

Allison nodded. "Sure. I'll use the ice from my drink." She laughed.

I guess it was hearing Allison's laugh. Suddenly I missed all the times we'd had together.

"Hey, Ali," I said, "I'm sorry."

"Me too. I should have said it first."

Most of our words were drowned out by the junior high band. But I could tell by the smile on Allison's face that we'd both heard enough to go back to being best friends.

Finally, except for the drummer, the band left the stage. There was a loud, earsplitting squeal over the public-address system as Mr. Delvechio strode across the stage.

"Ladies and gentlemen. Boys and girls. Honored guests." Mr. Delvechio's voice rang throughout the shopping center. "There are two prizes. The grand prize winner will receive an all-expenses-paid trip for two to Disney World. The second prize is for the runner-up. If for any reason, the grand prize winner cannot use the prize or if the entry is disqualified, then the runner-up becomes the grand prize winner." Taking a deep breath, Mr. Delvechio reached inside his pocket. He pulled out the pink-and-brown envelope as the drum began to roll.

"Don't take all day," Mike Pierce shouted.

Appearing not to hear, Mr. Delvechio slowly tore open the envelope. He unfolded the paper and wiped the sweat from his forehead. "And the runner-up is . . ."

Another drumroll.

"Stephanie Kulik."

I heard nothing but screams. Mom was holding on to both of my shoulders and jerking me up and down, rattling my brains. All around me people started thumping my back. Allison gave me a big hug while kids who rarely talked to me in school were calling, "Way to go, Steph!" And I didn't even know what I'd won yet.

Suddenly I felt a push. I was supposed to go up front. I was supposed to walk across the stage in front of everyone.

I heard the kids calling for me. They were clapping in rhythm to my name. "Steph. Steph. Steph."

Impossible. My knees had turned to mush and my stomach had never felt so queasy. But somehow I managed to move toward the stage, aware of the hundreds of eyes all focused on me.

The clapping turned to a roar as my foot touched the stage. A jet plane couldn't have been louder.

"Ladies and gentlemen," Mr. Delvechio's voice again boomed into the microphone. "I want you to know that this lovely lady has won her prize over three hundred other entrants. That's right. There were three hundred other entrants, only one of which was judged better than hers. And a winning flavor it was too. Stephanie, do you want to tell the good people out there what the name of your flavor is?"

I guessed Mr. Delvechio must have seen from the sick expression on my face that I was in no condition to speak. Besides, I'd plain forgotten. Being the kind person he was, Mr. Delvechio continued.

"Stephanie's being modest, folks. The originality of Stephanie's flavor impressed me. Even its name is creative and definitely appropriate: Chocolate Daze. D-a-z-e," he announced. "A rare concoction of chocolate that is sure to put chocolate lovers everywhere into a chocolate daze. I couldn't have invented anything more delicious myself."

Mr. Delvechio waited for the applause to die down.

"Now, what I have for you, Stephanie, is a gift certificate for two hundred dollars' worth of ice cream from my store. Thanks for entering my contest."

As I left the stage, the drumroll began again, this time for the winner of the grand prize, the trip to Disney World. I was close enough to see Mike lean forward. I had to bite my lip. Part of me still didn't want him to win, but not too big a part. I'd done my best. Maybe Mike had too.

"And now . . ." As Mr. Delvechio paused, Mike glanced up and caught my eye.

Then I did something I never would have thought possible. I crossed my fingers for Mike and held them up for him to see. When Mike smiled and crossed his fingers in a signal back to me, I could tell he was grateful the war was finally over.

". . . the grand prize winner is . . . Howard Woodward."

Silence. Absolute silence. The announcement left

everyone in the audience stunned. Who was Howard Woodward? No one came forward.

"Hey, that's not fair," someone yelled. "Doesn't the winner have to be here to get the prize?"

"I never even heard of a Howard Woodward," someone else called. "Who the heck is he?"

"Yeah, and what was his flavor?" someone close to the stage wanted to know.

"Who cares? That prize should be Stephanie's."

I almost dropped dead in my tracks. That was Mike telling everyone I should win the trip to Disney World!

As I made my way back to where Mom and Allison were standing, I could feel a general rumble building in the audience. Someone started to clap and chant my name. Others picked it up, and the sound grew louder and louder.

I bent my head, covered my face with my hands, and burrowed against Mom's side. I knew the rules as well as Mr. Delvechio. Still, it felt good knowing the kids and people in my town wanted me to be their grand prize winner.

Gradually the clapping died down as Mr. Delvechio tapped the microphone. He read from the rule sheet what I already knew: that the winner did not have to be present or even living here in order to win the prize. Howard Woodward had apparently been visiting from New York when he entered the contest. Mr. Delvechio would call and notify him of his prize.

A few boys whistled their disapproval, and I heard a few boos. Then it was over.

After the celebration, Mom and I ended up at the new park and playground a couple of blocks from the shopping center. As we walked along the garden path, I could see the ladies in the garden club had been busy. All the rosebushes were mulched high with wood chips, and most were coming out of their winter dormancy. All had shiny metal stakes with names like Peace or Tranquility. You would really have to look to find a weed or a piece of trash. Daffodils bobbed their heads in the gentle breeze.

In the distance I could hear the crack of a baseball bat as it connected with a ball. In a couple of weeks the Little League season would begin. I was thinking that maybe it was as my mother said: Growing up was a lot like riding the elevator to the top of the Washington Monument and looking out the window. From there you could see everything more clearly than on the ground. What she meant, I'd come to find out, was that sometimes you didn't know how dumb something was until after it was all over.

I guessed that was how it was with my dad and me and trying to get Mom and him back together again. It just wasn't going to work. Anyway it was their marriage, not mine. I was just the kid who happened to be involved.

We found a bench and sat down.

"You know what I like about daffodils?" Mom said.

"What?" I was sure she'd say it was the color. Yellow was her favorite too.

"The way they come up year after year. I always feel good when I see them in the spring. It tells me another year's gone by. I'm still here, and you're still here, and we're absolutely making it together."

I didn't say anything. I leaned my head against her shoulder and took another lick of ice cream.